Beautiful Misfits Press

hello@beautifulmisfitspress.com

Publisher's Note: This is a work of fiction. All names, characters, locations, and incidents are products of the author's imagination. Locales and public names are sometimes used for atmospheric purposes. Any resemblance to actual persons, things, living or dead, or to businesses, companies, events, institutions, or locales is entirely coincidental.

Edited By: Editing by Kimberly Dawn

Cover Design: Wildheart Graphics

Cover Image: Concepts by Canea

SURVIVING THE HOLLY-DAYS / Echo Grayce. — 1st ed.

Sit Still, Look Pretty • Daya
The Man • Taylor Swift
Faster • Matt Nathanson
Sleeping With A Friend • Neon Trees
Closer • Tegan and Sara
Sugar, We're Goin Down • Fall Out Boy
One More Night • Maroon 5
Dirty Little Secret • The All-American Rejects
Into You • Ariana Grande
Everything Has Changed • Taylor Swift, Ed Sheeran
Mistletoe And Holly • Javier Barrera
A Symptom Of Being Human • Shinedown
Stargazing • Myles Smith
Carry You Home • Alex Warren
If You Love Her • Forest Blakk
Come On Get Higher • Matt Nathanson
Run • Matt Nathanson, Sugarl.
I Lived • OneRepublic
Slow Hands • Niall Horan
Geronimo • Sheppard

Echo Grayce

Classic • MKTO
Brave • Sara Bareilles
If I Were a Boy • Beyoncé
Stand By You • Rachel Platten
I Can Do It With a Broken Heart • Taylor Swift
Hit Me With Your Best Shot • Pat Benatar
White Winter Hymnal • Pentatonix
A Bar Song (Tipsy) • Shaboozey
Just A Kiss • Lady A
I Don't Wanna Be In Love • Good Charlotte
Bang a Gong (Get It On) • T. Rex
Vibes • SIX60
Shivers • Ed Sheeran
Dress • Taylor Swift
The Only Exception • Paramore
Breakin' Dishes • Rihanna
Underneath the Mistletoe • Sia
Too Much • Dove Cameron
Girl On Fire • Alicia Keys
Story of My Life • One Direction
History • One Direction
Chasing Cars • Snow Patrol
All In • Lifehouse
Everything • Lifehouse
Between The Raindrops • Lifehouse, Natasha
Bedingfield
Most Girls • Hailee Steinfeld
Snow On The Beach • Taylor Swift, Lana Del Rey
Still Into You • Paramore
Man! I Feel Like A Woman! • Shania Twain

Surviving the Holly-Days

Sweet Caroline • Neil Diamond
I Was Made For Lovin' You • YUNGBLUD
Fight Song • Rachel Platten
You're On Your Own, Kid • Taylor Swift

Want the bangers??? Get them here
geni.us/HollyDaysBangers

For Samantha, Aries, and Bronwyn...

Never make yourself small.
Never make excuses for
mediocre men.
Keep standing up for those who can't
stand for themselves.
Take up space.
Be loud. Be too much.
And never fucking apologize one single time
for it.
You are the best things
I've ever done.
Fuck my books. Fuck my cover art.

You're the mark I'm leaving
on the world.
Keep calling them on their shit.

Blaze the fucking trail.

And know every single minute, you're making
the world a better place.

~Mom

I

Holly

Every bit of zen I try to channel evaporates on a frustrated growl at the sound of my brother's smooth, recorded voice for the third time.

"Nick, I swear to God, if you forgot—" The automated voicemail cuts me off mid-rant.

A sharp twinge pulses behind my left eye—nature's warning shot that a migraine is locked and loaded.

Thanks, Santa. Really feeling that Christmas magic.

Right now, I'd take a sleigh full of reindeer shit over the ice pick about to jam itself in my skull.

My fifth voicemail in twenty minutes hits his inbox with the fury of a woman stuck in purgatory. "Nicholas Andrew McAdams, I don't care if you're dead in a ditch. It's not an acceptable excuse for—"

The automated system cuts me off.

Again.

I spin in place, my heels squeaking against the terminal floor as I scan for something—anything at all. A forgotten customer service rep. A sympathetic janitor. Hell, I'll take a therapy dog at this point.

One look at the time tells me customer service is closed. According to the sign overhead, the next flight won't arrive for another three hours.

From Chicago.

Great.

For my sanity, I forgo calling one more time and switch to text.

ME

You better not have left me here.

Delivered.

ME

Cute how "delivered" keeps popping up when I'm literally NOT delivered anywhere.

Delivered.

ME

Fair warning... Santa's not the only one making a list. And your balls just made the naughty one

Delivered.

ME

Hope you're practicing your high notes, because I'm about to turn you into a Christmas castrato. Deck your halls with that ♫

Delivered.

ME

Silent Night is about to get real literal for you, buddy.

When my phone finally buzzes… it's not Nick's face on the screen, but my mother's. Probably calling to critique my travel outfit or remind me to pack my "gathering-appropriate" underthings.

Because God forbid the queen sees a panty line during family photos.

I let it go to voicemail and slump against the wall, watching the arrival board flicker like a horror movie jump scare. One by one, each incoming flight status transforms to CANCELED in festive, sadistic red.

At this point, my brother forgetting to pick me up would be the glitter-bombed middle finger of the night. Trust the golden boy to handle one simple task without—

"Haaaavvvvve a holly jolly…"

The terminal's speaker system that had been playing sedate instrumental music kicks it up a notch, Frank Sinatra's festive croon suddenly blaring at full volume.

Well, *Frank*, Holly is not freaking jolly. Holly is so

devoid of jolly, *Fraaaaank,* she might actually murder someone with a candy cane.

With the single most important moment of my life looming just days away, this is the single worst time for my luggage to flit off to Narnia.

Boston to Portland. One flight. Fifty minutes. How the hell did the airline screw this up?

My luggage probably found the first bar and sidled right up to all the other things missing in my life—my favorite fuzzy sock, the Tupperware lid I used exactly once, my pride after taking an unfortunate ride on my ex, and my newfound confidence after nailing my last proposal.

Confidence I desperately need to get through my upcoming presentation.

The one at the lodge during our annual Christmas McAllister/McAdams mashup.

Head-to-head against my father and the company he built from the ground up and still lords over to this day.

The one I want him to pass to me.

You know, if I can get him to stop seeing the bubbly daydreamer I used to be. The one who cranked her music too high, wore her quirky clothes too bright, and laughed too loud.

Okay, I still do that when I'm not in the office. If the music is too loud, well, he's just too damn old. How about that?

Too much. He's always seen me as too much. And sure, I'm probably a Roman candle next to my brother,

Nick, but I've mastered the art of buttoned-up-executive me from nine to five, careful to avoid Elle Woods territory with her glam-infused professional chic style dipped in signature pink.

Unfortunately, the overachiever I am, I shot right past driven, fresh executive territory and skidded straight into some Stepford Wife twilight zone.

Basically, a walking uterus of good breeding who's prettier when she smiles.

Gag.

What a waste of my perfectly lovely charm.

You'd think my nauseating professionalism in the wardrobe department would give me some clout as a grown woman, right?

No.

And now I'm a grown woman with no clout… and without my freaking wardrobe.

Glaring at the empty, unmoving belt, I check my phone one more time.

This is the kick in the tits I do not need.

No. *No!* I refuse to believe my bag didn't make it. There's no way. My manifestation panties would not do me dirty by gallivanting off to some horny happy hour in Narnia.

A flash of movement behind the clear rubber flaps leading to the inner sanctum catches my eye. The only sign of life in this place.

My only hope. My saving grace. My own Christmas miracle?

Dropping my phone onto my carry-on, I glance around, say goodbye to my dignity, and hike up my skirt.

The minute I drop to my hands and knees—Jesus, could this be any more humiliating—I hear my mother's voice in my head.

"That's not very ladylike, dear."

Get used to it, Mother… I'm the very picture of a modern career woman getting shit done.

I flinch with every grind of the metal plates against my knees. Biting my lip, I barely hold back the string of curses begging to be set free and wonder again how I got here.

Bruised knees from savoring a well-endowed dick with my tongue? No.

Rug burn earned riding that mythical dick reverse cowgirl? Pfffft.

Nope… my impending black and blue knees are a direct result of my desperation.

Shoving through the thick, heavy rubber flaps reeking of oil and dust, I flail my arm, keeping it totally sexy, but hey, if it gets the job done. Excuse me?"

A good twenty feet away and surrounded by the hum of machinery, the whir of fans, and muffled tunes, the guy I spotted continues to adjust carts. Metal scrapes against concrete as he works, his back turned, completely ignoring my presence.

Just as he's about to disappear out of sight behind conveyor belts and machinery, my heart leaps into my throat on a wave of panic.

With two fingers between my lips—a move that

would have my mother clutching her pearls—I let loose a piercing whistle that echoes off the concrete walls. "Hey!"

My mother hated Nick and Chance teaching me something so crude, insisting the idea of me ever needing the skill was absolutely unthinkable.

Nick and Chance - 1. Mom - 0.

The guy's head snaps around so fast it practically qualifies him for workman's comp, his safety vest swinging with the motion.

Disinterested eyes narrow in a glare beneath the brim of his neon orange beanie. "What the hell?"

I straighten my spine, well, as much as one can when they're on their hands and knees, refusing to be intimidated. "My bag… it never made it out."

He crosses his arms, his safety vest pulling tight across his chest. "And what does that tell you?"

I match his bored expression. "That you're incompetent."

"Lady, all of the bags on the flight were unloaded." He gestures at the empty carousel behind me with a dismissive wave. "If it's not out there, it didn't make it on the plane in Boston. Now get off the belt."

I resist the urge to shift on my knees and maintain my hard stare. "Check. Again."

His jaw ticks. "I don't have to. There's no more luggage back here. There is a booster seat. Yours?"

"Do you really want to have to deliver it to me three hours away tomorrow?"

"I don't deliver bags." He kicks at a stray piece of paper on the ground and snorts. "Besides, I'm off tomorrow."

"Cute. You know what I mean."

His eyes drop from my face in a slow, deliberate slide, his attention landing somewhere in the vicinity of my cleavage with all the finesse of a drunk frat boy at last call.

The corner of his mouth curls up. "What do you want me to do, whip out my magic wand and alakazam it here?"

And there it is—the eyebrow waggle. The universal signal of male mediocrity that keeps Charlie's sex toy party side gig thriving.

Why did all guys turn into pigs who thought they had the power to fix all of our problems with a sixty-second ride on their underwhelming dicks?

"Next you're going to make some nine and three-fourths reference. How original. And"—I peruse him from head to toe, my lip curling— "optimistic of you."

His grin slips and his eyes narrow, two red splotches forming on his cheeks. "You know what your problem is?"

I tap my chin in mock thought. "Aw, a classic from the *Old Testament of The Complete Idiot's Guide to Never Getting Laid*. You might want to check out the *New Testament*—I hear they've upgraded it from when shoulder pads were considered power moves."

He takes a menacing step forward, his work boots

scuffing on concrete. "Listen, princess, why don't you go back to your first-class lounge and let the adults handle this? I'm sure daddy's credit card can replace whatever's in that missing bag."

My fingernails dig crescents into my palm as his words land exactly where he aimed them. "That bag has my entire future in it. I swear to God——"

"What the hell do you think you're doing, Squirt?"

The deep baritone slices through the terminal's chaos, and every cell in my body stands at attention. That damn voice. So familiar, yet somehow grittier, more dominant—*nope*, commanding, *blurgh*—than I remember, rolls through me. A shiver starts at my nape and cascades down my spine, leaving a trail of goose-bumps behind while an unwelcome heat blooms in my chest.

Anyone but him, dammit.

My brother's best friend—and the only man who's ever pushed me to the opposite extremes of wanting to climb him like a tree and throat punch him—looms somewhere behind me.

Of course GI Joe would catch me like this—on my knees, fighting with airport personnel.

The universe has a sick sense of humor.

I resist the urge to snap at him because I know exactly what I'll find when I turn around. Six feet plus of sculpted Army perfection hugged by cargo pants, a Henley that hides nothing, and disapproval.

And I'm definitely not ready to face the one man

who's always made me feel simultaneously too much and not enough—especially on my knees.

My life is officially a Hallmark movie directed by Satan.

2
CHANCE

Things I expect to find walking into Portland International to pick up Holly McAdams:

A trail of stunned businessmen who mistook her pink lipstick for weakness instead of the war paint it is.

Relentless muttering about market projection formulas, risk analysis ratios, sprinkled between pop song one-liners like some kind of tiny financial guerrilla warrior with a built-in soundtrack.

Even state-of-emergency level destruction from the frenetic cyclone on heels sweeping through everyone and everything in her path.

What I do not expect is to find her on her hands and knees, pert little ass in the air, her damn head shoved through the baggage claim flaps, and that tiny pencil skirt riding up, revealing smooth, toned thighs as she argues with airport personnel, her voice carrying across the terminal.

What in the—*Jesus Christ.*

I should intervene. I should absolutely step in and handle this situation with the calm, strategic precision the Army drilled into me. But nah—this is Holly, and I'm on vacation.

Instead, I pull out my phone, a shit-eating grin spreading across my face. I have a best friend to pay back for saddling me with his sister-sitting duties while *he's* playing house with *my* sister, Charlie.

The one he was not supposed to diddle but diddled anyway last Christmas. And in a particularly cheap kick to the balls, he sent me a damn pic of her with her freshly fucked glow in a goddamn lip-lock with him.

I'm delivering brutal payback until the kids—the ones they don't have yet—go to college.

ME

[image attached] I'm charging you a handling fee. This was not part of the plan

NICK

What the hell is she doing?

ME

Giving everyone a show while she threatens baggage claim personnel. Gonna need to add hazard pay to that fee

NICK

Get her off her knees!

ME

That's what she said

NICK

When I get my hands on you, you're a
dead man

ME

Death by Holly seems more likely. Rabid
little thing. I'll send you the med bills

NICK

I'm serious.

ME

Nice to meet you, Serious   I'm your
sister's new handler. Want to help me
pick out a collar and leash for her.

NICK

Get her out of there dammit.

ME

On it, Captain Killjoy. My squad of
one is moving in.

NICK

Don't call me that. You know I hate it.
And keep your damn hands off my sister.

ME

Me? I'm just a humble soldier following
orders. Wait, which orders am I following
again?

NICK

Chance, I swear to God, if you...

ME

Relax, Nick. I got this 😕 Your baby sis is in good hands. *glances at photo again* Though maybe not the best position... 😬 I'll get her straightened out. Literally and figuratively 😏

NICK

Listen Prick, I'm trusting you. Heading to Charlie's. If you don't hear from me... just get her out of there before she ends up in jail or worse.

ME

🫡 Yes, sir! Consider it done. Though a little jail time might do Squirt some good... 😈

"Listen, princess, why don't you toddle back to your first-class lounge and let the adults handle this?"

And there it is, the little princess dig, dripping with condescension. This asshole doesn't know who he's messing with.

The employee's patronizing tone sets off every protective instinct I've got, like a trip wire rigged to my protective big brother reflex.

My amusement evaporates as I shove my phone in my pocket.

With my jaw set, my laser-focus gaze snaps to the unfolding situation, assessing the threat level.

Some things never change. She's still that same spit-fire who used to pick fights with anyone who underestimated her or dared tell her what she could or couldn't do. Only now she does it in a pencil skirt that's clearly designed to short-circuit a man's defenses and turn his brain to static.

"That bag has my entire future in it. I swear to God—"

Her voice is low and dangerous, carrying a warning growl I've never quite heard from her before.

One that immediately makes me think of anger-fueled sex.

My brain skids to a halt harder than a private face-planting during a morning PT session.

I'm not thinking of her that way. It's just leftover energy from giving Nick shit. That's all. Nothing more.

A familiar restlessness I haven't experienced in a hot minute skitters along my skin, all prickling heat.

Because I'm an idiot.

An idiot who probably should have skipped our annual family Christmas trip for a second year in a row and taken the time to find some willing company to scratch this particular itch.

Pipe the fuck down, libido. No need for blood to be pumping hot and heavy to my junk like a busted hydrant in July. We're here for family bonding, not a Hallmark Channel holiday hookup. The last thing I need is to be walking around with a hair trigger, ready to blow at the first glimpse of Holly, of all people, in a tight sweater or short skirt.

"What the hell do you think you're doing, Squirt?" The words are out, laced with the bite of frustration, before I can stop them. The nickname slips off my tongue with practiced ease.

More than two decades of calling her that, and suddenly it feels wrong in my mouth. Because the woman I haven't laid eyes on in two years—the one whose spine just went ramrod straight at the sound of my voice—is definitely not the kid sister I remember.

I blame the skirt. And the legs. And the way she's practically vibrating with that familiar stubborn, defiant energy that always spelled trouble, like a live wire sparking and spitting.

The image sears itself into my brain, taunting me. She's never allowed to vibrate while on her hands and knees again.

I'm supposed to get her to the lodge in one piece. Getting her there unfucked was an unspoken condition to those orders, but right now, watching her slowly turn to face me with fire in her narrowed baby blues, I'm starting to think I'm the one who's fucked.

"Fucking hell."

Airport security doesn't take kindly to civilians breaching restricted areas, even pint-sized ones in fuck-me pencil skirts.

"Up. Now," I mutter through clenched teeth as I half haul her up to her feet before she gets herself arrested for disorderly conduct.

She yanks free the second she's vertical, but not before I catch her wobbling in those ridiculous heels. "My entire presentation is in that damn bag. Bound proposals. Risk analysis spreadsheets—this, THIS is why

I never should have let Derek convince me to pack them in my checked bag to 'help me relax' on the plane. Forced relaxation, my ass."

"Who the hell is Derek?" The question flies out of my mouth unchecked, sharp and demanding. Not that I care. I'm just trying to assess the situation. Gather intel. Know thy enemy and all that.

"Does it matter? The point is, I need my goddamn suitcase." Her eyes flash, her chin jutting forward stubbornly. Classic Holly, digging in her heels.

"Look, you can verbally flay customer service from the safety of my truck." I nod toward the windows where fat wet snowflakes cling to the glass. "But we need to move. Now."

"I am not leaving without—"

"Your personal brand of chaos? Already packed, Squirt." I eye the sky-high stilettos that probably cost more than my truck payment. "Though common sense clearly didn't make the cut."

Her eyes narrow to slits. "Says the guy whose entire Call of Duty cosplay signature look just stepped out of a two-for-one special at Tactical Bros 'R' Us. Tell me more about how cargo pants are appropriate for every occasion, GI Jackass. Don't worry, I'll wait while you check all sixteen pockets for your comeback."

"Definitely rabid." Before she can process my words, I duck down and throw her over my shoulder in a fireman's carry, her startled yelp music to my ears.

"Put me down!" She pounds her tiny fists against my

back, her hits landing without any real force. "I swear to God, I will make you regret—"

Stomping the twenty feet toward the exit, I resign myself to the special circle of hell that will be three long hours stuck in a confined space with her and her endless feral energy.

My immediate future a whole lot like climbing into a trap with a wild, possibly rabid raccoon.

Nick owes me big time.

Wind as biting as her temper greets us the minute we step outside, sending a thick wall of snow swirling around us all but swallowing us whole.

The second my boot makes contact with the icy ground, we're sliding. Without thinking, I adjust my grip, my palm sliding dangerously high up her thigh as I fight for balance.

"Hands!" she squeaks, squirming against my shoulder.

The snow sticking to the asphalt makes the trek to my truck look like a drunken three-legged race waiting to happen.

"Maybe next time pack some clothes suitable for, oh, I don't know… Maine in December." I hitch her higher on my shoulder, definitely not thinking about how soft and warm her skin is under my palm. Or how if I move it just a fraction more, my index finger will find a new home in the crease between her taut little ass cheek and thigh. "Now stop squirming, unless you want us both to end up on our asses."

"I had weather-appropriate clothes, you dickhead."

She grumbles, her voice muffled against my back, hot breath seeping through my shirt.

The heat of it, of her, bleeds into me, and I can't say I entirely hate it, my treacherous body reacting in all sorts of inappropriate ways.

I've never been more grateful for my Army training, for the discipline that allows me to ignore even the most tempting distractions, no matter how good they feel… or sound… or how incredible they smell, like vanilla sugar cookies and something uniquely Holly.

Razzing Nick via text aside, I'm not actually going there. Don't shit where you eat. Don't piss in your own foxhole. Never muddy your own trench. No matter how you slice it, this little ski vacation is our own proverbial foxhole, our shared trench, and with a built-in audience watching our every move like hawks.

One lingering look, one suspicious touch, is all it takes to set the family gossip mill ablaze. And while I'm all for living dangerously, I prefer my risks of the enemy combatant variety, not the familial warfare one.

Reaching my truck at last, I yank open the passenger door and unceremoniously dump her into the seat, her skirt riding up to reveal a flash of white lace. "Now try to control both your mouth and your skirt, Squirt, and buckle up."

She rolls her eyes skyward and smirks. "I need to call customer service."

"Skirt. Seat belt. Customer service. In that order, genius."

She complies with an air of affronted dignity,

smoothing her disheveled hair and yanking the seat belt into place with a little more force than necessary. Her flushed cheeks and wild, windswept waves are the picture of feminine outrage—a deeply fuckable picture that I shouldn't be noticing.

"Fine. But I'm putting the call on speaker. So lay off the orders."

"As long as we get on the road sometime today, I don't give a flying fuck. Knock yourself out, Squirt." I slam her door with more oomph than necessary before circling to the driver's side as I give myself a much-needed mental shake.

This is Nick's little sister.

This is also all Nick's fault.

If he hadn't hooked up with Charlie last Christmas, I wouldn't think of Holly as anything other than the same pain in the ass wild child who used to follow us around and pester us incessantly, trying to hang with the big boys.

As I slide behind the wheel, I cast a sideways glance at the fuming brunette bedside me. "It's a vacation, Hols, not a working holiday. Remember? Skiing, booze, bad decisions we'll all claim not to remember in the morning?"

Her lips curve into a smile that's anything but sweet. "Maybe for you, GI Jackass. Some of us have bigger plans. Now shut up and drive."

"Sir, yes, sir," I mutter, cranking the engine. It's going to be a long three hours. A really long three hours. But as I pull out of the airport lot, her fingers already flying furiously over her phone screen, I can't help the small grin tugging at my mouth.

Same old Holly. Pretty, prickly, and ready to take on the world, one overpriced stiletto at a time. If I play my cards right, this forced quality time will be just what we need to get back on solid ground.

As long as I can keep my hands to myself, my smart-ass comments in check, and my dick in line, it'll be smooth sailing.

How hard can it be?

3
Holly

"We're sorry, but all representatives are currently assisting—"

"Bullshit!" I've seen what they consider assisting and again… bullshit. I stab the red button on my phone with way more force than necessary, resisting the urge to chuck it out the window into the swirling snow. The automated system cuts off mid-apology for what has to be the twentieth time, my signal fading in and out like my patience.

Beside me, Chance's jaw flexes. He drums his fingers against the steering wheel while his eyes narrow, fixed on the wall of white ahead of us. The storm that started as pretty, pillowy snowflakes has morphed into a full-blown whiteout.

My phone chirps as another bar of service flickers to life. It's a trap. I know it's a trap. Fate wants me to try one more time so she can smack me right in the ego—and maybe a little south of it, just to keep things spicy.

Don't threaten me with a good time. It's been a damn minute since I... got properly spun around and left breathless. The sit and spin was just the gateway toy.

I dial again, praying to whatever deity handles lost luggage and automated customer service lines to please, please just let me file a claim.

"Welcome to—" The mechanical voice crackles, breaks up, then dies completely.

Gee, who didn't see that coming?

With a deep breath that does absolutely nothing to calm my rising anxiety, I fire off a text to Charlie.

ME

Storm's getting worse. Might have to stop.

Her reply is immediate...

CHARLIE

•• Just you and GI Joe?

ME

Don't start.

CHARLIE

Maybe you'll get lucky and there'll only be one room left...

ME

Not all of us throw our cat at our brother's best friend after one night of sharing a bed.

CHARLIE

Best decision I ever made though

ME

Gross. In my mind, my brother has no dick. I refuse to believe otherwise.

CHARLIE

I hate to break it to you, but not only does he have a dick, he's packing a in those jeans.

ME

Is that a bat? Why the hell did you drop a bat emoji?

CHARLIE

I couldn't find a baseball bat so I had to improvise.

ME

OMG, staaaahhhhpppp. We are NOT you. He can be smuggling a cannon between his legs for all I care. If we have to stop, we're handling it like adults.

CHARLIE

Gurrrlllll… I'll have you know, I was very adult when I sexually harassed your brother with my mega wand.

ME

I hate you.

CHARLIE

Hey, I can't help it if he gives good
And what he can do with the is

A gust of wind rocks the truck. Pure instinct has me throwing out my hands to brace myself. The one gripping the door handle—smart move. The one gripping Chance's rock-hard thigh—not so much.

"As much as I enjoy your aggressive approach to stress relief, Squirt, maybe find a different gear shift to grab." His voice drops an octave, a dangerous rumble that definitely doesn't make my stomach flip. "You're not tall enough to ride this ride."

"Trust me, soldier boy, if I wanted to ride anything in this truck, I'd start with your ego—seems like that's the biggest thing in here."

The charged air between us crackles with tension. Chance's jaw clenches, a muscle ticking beneath the shadowed scruff lining his chiseled features. He takes a slow, measured breath, like he's mentally counting to ten.

Or twenty.

When the truck lurches, he mutters something that sounds suspiciously like a prayer under his breath.

Knuckles white with the force of his grip, he squints through the windshield.

I'm all for living dangerously, but when the speedometer starts giving me side-eye at the idea of even attempting the reduced speed limit, I know it's time to tap out.

"That's it." His voice, rough with frustration, breaks the tense silence. "We're stopping."

Relief floods me even as my stomach does a weird flip-flop thing. Not because of spending the night with GI Jackass. Absolutely not. No fluttery feelings here. Just exhaustion and frustration over my lost clothes and… everything.

At the next exit, Chance pulls into a gas station and yanks his phone from one of his eight thousand tactical pockets—seriously, who needs that many pockets—and fires off a series of texts.

The blue light from his screen catches on that jaw— the one that should come with a warning label and liability waiver. Not that I'm looking. Or cataloging the way his shit-eating grin grows with every exchange like he's collecting frequent flyer miles in the Smug Airways rewards program.

I swear, the bromance between him and my brother is as if *Top Gun* and *Fight Club* had a love child—all testosterone, no chill. They're basically soulmates joined at the hip flask, bonded by their obsession with over-priced whiskey, carving up black diamonds, and a mutual hard-on for torturing their little sisters. I swear, these two were meant to share a womb… practicing their fist bumps and secret handshakes in utero.

His phone buzzes again, and this time his deep chuckle makes me wonder what that sound would feel like vibrating along the inside of my thigh.

"What's so funny?" I manage to ask like I'm not

currently imagining that voice doing very un-sisterly things to my nervous system.

"Your brother." He tilts the phone my way, and I catch a glimpse of their text chain, grateful for the distraction from my traitorous thoughts.

ME

Storm's brutal. Stopping for the night.

NICK

Keep it PG with my sister

ME

Hey, I can only control myself Who's going to tell her to keep it PG with me? Half an hour in a confined space and she already tried to put me in fifth gear

NICK

What? The? Fuck? Does? That? Mean?

ME

Gotta go my, dude I'll let you know when we head to bed—er, find a bed I mean, find a room

NICK

Dead man texting

ME

Relax We're not you guys. We can handle one night without shoving Tab A into Slot B

NICK

 is not slot B

ME

Hey, maybe she likes it in Slot C I wouldn't want to presume…

NICK

Whatever you shove in her Slot C, I shove in yours Remember that

ME

I wonder if Holly's more of a girl or maybe she's Olympic level

ME

Go big or go home, am I right?

NICK

Now, what the hell do those emojis mean?

ME

Go ask my sister, Old Man. She can help you with the lingo. I recommend a sedative first And maybe a medic standing by with a defibrillator.

"And there it is—" The words slip out before I can stop them. "Another guy who thinks slamming straight into fifth means he knows his way around a stick."

The darkness in the truck can't hide the way his jaw ticks. It's the same tell he's had since we were kids, the one that says I'm getting under his skin.

"Bold of you to assume I don't know my way around every gear in this truck, Squirt."

His voice hits me low in my belly, a direct strike that absolutely does not make me picture exactly how well he might know his way around things. I squeeze my thighs together and focus on the phone, because that's safer than acknowledging whatever just sparked between us.

I snort, falling back on the attitude that's gotten me through a lifetime of being underestimated. "Please. We are so not them."

"Exactly." His agreement comes too fast, too hard, like he's trying to outrun whatever's brewing between us. "We're…"

"Adults," I supply helpfully, definitely not watching the way his fingers drum against the leather of the steering wheel or how his forearms flex with each subtle movement. Nope. Not at all.

"Mature," he adds with a nod that holds about as much truth as my manifestation underwear's promise to make me 'fearless.'

Throwing the truck in gear, he eases back onto the road where the snow falls in unpredictable sheets with the precision of a drunk dart player.

"Yeah, super mature." My fingers dig into the edge of my seat as the bed of the truck fishtails in slow motion before catching grip again. "That's why you're sending my brother eggplant emojis and debating my sexual preferences. For someone who claims they're staying out of my slots, you sure had a lot to say about them."

The words fly out before I can stop them. Chance's grip on the wheel tightens. The muscle in his cheek jumps, the telltale tick that says I've gotten under his skin.

"Besides," I continue, unable to resist poking the

bear. "Anyone who sticks with the Tab A into Slot B routine is clearly working with training wheels. The real fun starts when you—never mind, I wouldn't expect GI Joe to know what to do with a girl who's into more than missionary anyway."

"Don't." The raw edge in his tone is a verbal shot of adrenaline straight to my bloodstream, sending a pulse of heat exactly where I don't need it, making me squirm in my seat.

The narrowed side-eye he aims at my lap tells me he definitely saw it. "Just… don't go there, Squirt."

The VACANCY sign at Wildwood Motor Lodge pulses through the snow in a steady red rhythm. The horseshoe-shaped building sprawls before us in all its vintage glory—the kind of place with exterior doors and metal keys, travel influencers would take selfies in front of and hashtag "authentic Americana."

If my mother knew I was about to stay at a motel where the doors open to the actual outdoors instead of climate-controlled hallways with crystal chandeliers, she'd need her prescription upped. A win-win. Sometimes being the family disappointment has its perks.

Chance pulls into a spot near the office, the heavy snow already starting to coat his windshield. "Stay here. I'll check us in."

"I'm perfectly capable of—"

"Of breaking your neck in those heels on the ice? Yeah, I know." He's already opening his door, letting in a blast of frigid air. "Just... stay put, Squirt. For once in your life, let someone else handle it."

I cross my arms and slump back in my seat, absolutely not watching the way his shoulders fill out his jacket as he trudges through the deepening snow.

The Army might have trained him to bark orders, but I stopped playing soldier the day my training bra got upgraded. Too bad my hormones never got the discharge papers, because they're still very much enlisted in whatever this is.

Ten minutes later, I'm bouncing on his damn shoulder again as he trudges through ankle-deep snow to room 112, the last one on the end. A rusty number hangs crooked on a door that's seen better decades.

Some clanking and three muttered curses later, the door finally swings open with an ominous creak. Craning my neck, my gaze lands on the bed.

One bed.

Of course, there's only one bed. A queen-size monstrosity covered in a floral print so aggressively retro it would make Austin Powers question his taste level.

"Well," I say into the loaded silence. "This is..."

"Mature?" Chance supplies helpfully, echoing our earlier conversation before he unceremoniously tosses me onto the center of the mattress.

I'm going to kill Charlie for jinxing us with her one-room prophecy. "Adult," I correct him. "We're adults. We can handle this."

"Keep telling yourself that, Squirt." He chuckles low as he heads for the door.

I push up onto my palms to face him, ready to unleash my sharp tongue, but the words die in my throat. Because Chance fills the doorway like every rom-com fantasy come to life, snowflakes melting in his hair, looking at me with an intensity that makes me forget why I ever thought sharing a room was a good idea.

Like maybe we're not as mature about this as we're pretending to be.

And maybe I don't want to be.

4
CHANCE

I should sleep in my fucking truck.

Hell, I've slept in worse conditions over my years in the Army. At least the truck has heat and no one forcing me to do pushups in the mud at ass o'clock in the morning.

And the damn booty temptress could keep her pert little ass right where I plopped her. Lying dead center of what has to be the comforter version of an ugly Christmas sweater. The print so bad it got kicked out of the competition and had to start its own support group. The thing probably plays "Jingle Bells" if you pat it hard enough.

I blame the emoji fest for this. The Tab A in Slot B or C successfully traumatized Nick, but the collateral damage is currently trying to bust through my zipper.

Mission objective: Success.

Collateral damage: Devastating.

Now, all I can think about is how she equated Tab A in slot B to some sort of amateur hour.

And the implication that she shed her training wheels a long time ago.

My fucking cock swelled against my zipper the minute the tinkling words rolled off her evil tongue. Like some hormone-driven cadet who can't maintain proper discipline.

No matter how many times I muttered, "Down boy," he continued to sit at attention in my fucking pants. Bypassing my common sense entirely. Court-martial worthy insubordination if I ever saw it.

Fuck.

And if I stay out here much longer, she'll be teetering her ass out here on those heels. Because Holly McAdams never met a battle she wouldn't charge into headfirst.

I grab my bags and trudge back toward my purgatory for at least the next twelve hours.

When I push through the door, I skid to a short stop. Holly's sprawled on her stomach across the bed, legs kicked up, ankles crossed, sucking on a Ring Pop while scrolling through her phone. The flash of white lace peeking out from under her hiked-up skirt short-circuits my brain.

"We should get you out of those wet clothes."

The wince is immediate.

Well, that's not how I meant for it to sound—tactical error number one.

The suggestive words hang there. Holly's full pink lips part in a way that invites… you know what… not fucking going there.

The vein in my temple throbs.

My dog in her bun, okay.

There. Fine. I went there.

In my head. And my little head.

I didn't go there out loud. That's all that matters. Small victories.

"I mean, I don't know what you've got in your carry-on, but if you don't—maybe you need—I've got a shirt you can borrow. If you want to—uh, need to."

The fuck is happening right now?

I sound like a fucking fifteen-year-old boy again, trying to fucking form a sentence after Sierra Barrett gave me my first hand job, right at the very lodge we're on our way to.

So much for military precision.

"Right. Because my clothes are currently living their best life somewhere between here and Boston." She flips open her bag and rummages through the contents. "I've got my laptop, three pairs of thigh-high fuzzy socks because priorities, and a spare pair of underwear for emergencies—though this wasn't exactly the emergency I had in mind. A water bottle covered in Taylor Swift lyrics, four different kinds of lip gloss, a Marty Moose *National Lampoon's Vacation* ornament, Nick's birthday present which is NOT breaking in transit, thankyouverymuch, my emergency supply of Red Bull, my entire stash of Ring Pops because adulting is hard, my collection of motivational sticky notes—seriously, don't judge —and… that's—looks like that's it. Nope, I lied. My glasses."

She draws the Ring Pop into her mouth before popping it back out with an obscene little smack and grins up at me. "So about that shirt…"

I grab my lucky flannel—the one piece of clothing that's seen me through three deployments—and watch her bounce on the balls of her perfectly arched feet all the way into the bathroom, taking every last ounce of my peace of mind with her. Nick's the son of a bitch who set this in motion, and he's going to pay for it.

The sisters weren't on our radar.

At all.

That was the bro code.

ME

The Pappy is on you until I'm dead

NICK

What if I die first?

ME

You better have made arrangements in the will to cover however many I suck down my gullet until I'm dead.

NICK

Talked to Charlie. Understand now the
emoji bombs you dropped. Thanks for
that asshole. Why don't you just kick me
in the balls for fuck's sake.

Kick him in the balls, huh… welp, he asked for it.

ME

Your wish is my command fucker. Did
you know Holly's luggage is MIA?

NICK

It's late... you wanna get to the point?

ME

She's wearing my shirt to bed

NICK

That's full-on porn for women, like gray
sweatpants. Don't even fucking joke
about that.

ME

Dude, porn is full-on porn for women.
Get with the times. The shirt is like a
fucking diamond. At least mine is. Now
back to that porn… I wonder how
flexible she is

NICK

I will end you. Slowly.

ME

Don't worry, my dude. I'll take good care
of her

NICK

One more word and I swear to God...

ME

In the interest of keeping a balanced diet… your sister=the food pyramid

NICK

You're dead to me. Actually dead.

ME

Good luck fucking my sister tonight while you're wondering if I'm fucking yours

She sings in the shower.

Off-key.

And her attempt at beatboxing? Makes my old drill sergeant's morning screech sound like a damn symphony.

Half an hour after she slipped into the bathroom, she steps out all freshly showered, ruining my life with the way she wears my favorite shirt.

In fifty years, they could ask me about the best piece of clothing I ever owned—and all I'll be able to recall is how she looks wearing it.

The way impossibly soft flannel swallows her from neck to knees, stripping away the chic businesswoman she is by day, transforming her into the goddamn girl next door everyone talks about, but no one can really define.

The one you want to scoop around the waist and drag against you while you fall asleep with your face nestled in the sweet-smelling, velvety skin of her neck.

Her hair curls at the ends, the tips brushing her rosy cheeks. Dipping her chin, she tucks her nose against my collar, her eyes drifting shut with her shaky inhale.

And just like that, my favorite shirt becomes the second most dangerous thing in the room.

5
Holly

My carefully curated executive armor dissolves the minute I slip into his shirt, and suddenly I'm just… Holly. Not the financial analyst. Not the perpetual little sister. Just me.

Drowning in—him.

The scent of pine needles and woodsmoke with something darker underneath, something distinctly Chance, envelops me. Every turn of the fabric sends another subtle wave to tease my senses as I roll up the sleeves. Pressing my nose to the collar, I inhale deeply.

Warmth floods my cheeks as his scent awakens something I thought I'd outgrown.

Like finding an old mixtape from a time when you fearlessly reached for the high, only wild young love can deliver, despite the inevitable crash-landing.

Stepping into a room that felt much bigger when I

wore more clothes now feels like stepping into an intimate dance. His heated gaze tracks my every move, igniting something dangerous. This shirt—oh, it has powers. Whether they're for good or for evil, I haven't decided yet. Right now? Pure hedonism.

It's not just breaking my carefully drawn rules—it's setting fire to my whole damn presentation.

No. Nope. Not going there. Not when I need every brain cell focused on winning this account.

Glancing away from his hot and wary stare, I dig my socks out of my bag. Red and white stripes because—candy canes.

If I have to be professional all day, my feet deserve to party. Some people have their little black dresses. I have my ridiculous socks.

They're my tiny act of rebellion against a world of gray suits, glass ceilings, and men who think a lack of dangly bits means a lack of business sense.

"So I've got this figured out," I announce in my desperation to break the tension. I stretch the stripes over my calves and smooth the plush knit over my knees. My fingertips tingle as nerves fire with every brush against my skin. No doubt from the two Red Bulls I downed on the plane.

That had to be it.

Definitely not because of how Chance looks sprawling in that chair, long legs stretched out, cargo pants hugging thick thighs in a way that makes my mouth run dry. The fabric pulls taut as he shifts, and I force my gaze away from the impressive display of muscle that comes from years of military training.

Chance's head snaps up from where he's pretending to be fascinated by the TV remote. Whatever he plans to say dies on his lips as his gaze tracks the movement of my hands. A muscle ticks in his jaw, his fingers flexing on the armrest like he's fighting to keep them there.

"Sleeping arrangements." I march over to the bed, my feet silent against the threadbare carpet, grateful my voice stays steady despite the way his gaze follows my every move.

"We sleep head-to-foot. That way, we each get our own blanket barrier, and it's not weird at all."

"Not weird at all," he echoes, but his voice has that rough edge again like a whiskey-soaked promise that should come with its own risk disclosure statement.

I settle cross-legged on the bed, pulling out my laptop. The familiar weight grounds me and reminds me why I'm here.

"I've got work to do anyway. Now that half of my materials are MIA, I need to put together a plan B in case I don't get my damn luggage back. Vaultress isn't exactly a client you wing it with."

His spine snaps straight. "Vaultress? Vaultress Global —the cybersecurity giant?"

I nod, watching his reaction carefully. Few people outside the industry realize just how significant they are. "You know them?"

"Hard not to. I'm a Cyber Operations Specialist." He leans forward, elbows on his knees, and something in his expression shifts from playful to serious. "They're setting industry standards right now. They're who everyone else is trying to catch up to."

"They have a staggering growth rate." Drumming my fingers against my laptop, I debate how much to tell him. Once the words are out, I can't stuff them back in. Right now, I have no audience for my failure. But I can't deny the appeal of someone else carrying the weight of my secret, someone capable of understanding what I'm up against.

"A growth rate with the potential to launch them into the stratosphere. Problem is, they could just as easily collapse. I vote stratosphere. But if they choose my father—"

"Wait?" Chance surges forward in his chair. "What does your father have to do with this?"

I trace the edge of my laptop, my nail catching on a scratch in the metal. "He's my competition."

The muscle in his jaw flexes as his eyes turn predatory. Like I just activated some dormant military protocol in his brain that's now recalibrating everything he thought he knew about this trip.

My voice comes out steadier than I feel. "He doesn't know yet. No one does."

The look he gives me is impossible to read—part admiration, part concern, all intensity. "Holly…"

"Don't." I throw up my hand. I've heard it all before, hundreds of times. But I've never heard it from him. And for reasons I absolutely will not be looking any closer at, I don't ever want to. "Don't tell me it's crazy. Or impossible. Or that I should just wait my turn."

"Actually," he says quietly, "I was going to ask why you don't just supersize the approach you know your father will take? Give them the 2.0 version."

A laugh bubbles up, but it's not entirely bitter. "Because that's not necessarily what they need. They think they want the most aggressive growth plan possible —they all do at first. But that's not how I work. I don't want to give them what they think they want; I want to give them what I know they want."

His eyebrows lift. "And how will you do that?"

I pull up my template, the familiar three-column structure centering me. "So, numbers don't tell the whole story. You have to watch people. Really watch them."

I glance up to find him studying me intently. The hitch in my breath is entirely coincidental.

"When I present options—steady growth, calculated risk, and what I call the 'dream big' scenario—I'm not just showing them projections. I'm learning who they are."

"How so?"

"Body language. Micro-expressions. Which slides entice them. Which make them shift in their seats." The words flow faster now, excitement building as I explain what makes me different—better—than the old guard. "Most of them don't actually know what they want until they see all the possibilities laid out. Until they understand what they'd have to sacrifice for each outcome."

"And your father doesn't work this way?"

"My father sees numbers as absolutes. Black and white. But people?" I shake my head. "People are all shades of gray."

Chance is quiet for a long moment. When he finally speaks, his words are measured. Careful. "What do you think he sees when he looks at you?"

The snort of derision is out before I can stop it. "When I try to show him what I can do, he only sees two possibilities. Either I'm his lily-white daughter marrying the right guy, having the exact right amount of babies, and throwing a mean dinner party for her husband's colleagues—or I'm the black sheep. The girl who wears concert tees and checkered Vans off the clock. The disappointment who'd rather land the account of the decade than land a husband who thinks like my father and would never consider planning the dinner party because it's his wife's job and beneath him."

Chance studies me for a long moment before speaking, his voice careful. "You know you're taking one hell of a risk."

"Sometimes the biggest risks have the biggest payoffs." I adjust my glasses, still unused to their weight after a day in contacts. "I just need one chance." My voice drops to barely a whisper. "One opportunity to prove I belong at the helm of his company and can take his legacy and make it even better."

"Be careful what you sacrifice to prove yourself, Holly. Trust me," he says quietly, tension threading through his words, "becoming what they want doesn't always work out the way you think it will."

Something flickers across his face—a shadow of old hurt I almost miss. Almost. I study him in the dim light, searching for more glimpses of that raw edge underneath. "You did it too, didn't you? Tried to be what someone wanted?"

He shifts in the chair, muscles bunching beneath his shirt. "Let's just say I made some choices. Trying to prove myself." His jaw works. "Ended up proving all the wrong things to all the wrong people."

"This isn't like that," I insist, but his words needle at something tender inside me. "I'm good at this, Chance. The numbers, the strategy, reading people—it's not just about proving something. It's who I am."

"And if your father can't see that?" The question lands soft but cuts deep. "If he's so busy looking for the next version of himself that he misses what's right in front of him—can you live with that?"

"I already am." The words scrape past the lump in my throat. "At least I'll know I tried. That I didn't let him have the final say on my worth."

He nods, something shifting in his expression. "Then it's time to make sure that presentation is bulletproof."

An hour later, my eyes burn from reviewing slides, but my strategy feels solid. Maybe even unshakeable. I close my laptop, darkness swallowing us whole, and reach for my phone. One quick Google search later—

"You're a penetration tester???"

He lets out a low groan. "Christ, Squirt… aren't you tired?"

"Yes, but now I have questions, and you have answers." The mattress squeaks as I sit up straighter, suddenly wide awake.

"We use the term pen testers."

"Oh, I'm sure you do." I bite back a grin. "Doesn't change the fact that you're definitely a professional penetrator."

He heaves an exasperated sigh. Or maybe it's the sound of his surrender. He's known me my whole life. He has to know he's not getting out of this.

"You're not giving this up anytime soon, are you?"

And there it is. The resignation of a man who knows he's cornered. "Not a chance. What's the accident rate in your line of work? Do you have early withdrawal penalties?"

"Holly…"

The warning in his voice only eggs me on. His resistance is just another asset to leverage. "Remember what I said about training wheels? I ditched mine a long time ago, at the bottom of an ocean of tequila, but that's a story for another day."

His teeth grind loud enough for me to hear, followed by a muttered, "Goddammit."

"Probably a story for a different audience too."

A few seconds later, his exasperated, "Jesus, not again."

Whatever that means.

"If you don't paint me a picture, I'll just have to use my imagination."

He scoffs. SCOFFS. "I'm not worried. I've seen your art. Stick figures on the back of junk mail—and that's being generous."

"Wow, GI Jackass, I actually have to give you credit for that one."

"I thought that might shut you up."

"Guess again, bunk buddy. Wanna hear a fun fact?"

"I'm pretty sure the correct answer is hell no."

"Too bad. I value a well-rounded education. So did you know…"

"I'm already dreading this."

The ancient heater decides it's the right time to knock and wheeze to life, drowning out my words.

Suuuuuurrrrreeeeee, take his side.

"As I was saying… did you know, if you were born naturally, the first vajay you had your mouth on was your mother's."

"Dammit, woman. You're going to cause a medical condition saying shit like that."

"A boner killer, am I right?"

"That would be the condition."

"Technically, this particular cause of ED would fall under psychological conditions."

"As does this conversation."

"Okay, mind scrub time. Do you think having your head at the foot of the bed is like picking tails in heads or tails?"

The laugh that bursts from him is pure sin wrapped in velvet—deep, rich, and completely unfair.

It vibrates through me like the raw, potent bass sounds at a Fall Out Boy concert, settling low in my belly and spreading outward until my skin tingles.

It's the kind of laugh that makes you want to catalog every possible way to hear it again, preferably while he's hovering over you, his breath hot against your neck…

The mattress shifts as he settles in with his head at the foot of the bed. Silence fills the darkness, and despite the mattress under us being old enough to have RSVP'd to Woodstock, my muscles relax. Something about my inability to make out his features makes me brave.

Or maybe just honest.

"What if I'm not enough?" The whispered words slip out before I can stop them. My heart pounds in my ears as the seconds tick by with no reply.

Maybe he's asleep.

He has to be asleep.

Because if he doesn't think I'm enough, I don't— I can't—

Warm fingers find mine in the dark, his calloused hand sliding against my own.

The ache building in my chest slinks away like a coward in the face of this soldier's quiet strength.

"You see yourself with remarkable clarity, Holly." His voice is quiet but firm. "Don't start doubting that now. That's enough."

I swallow the massive lump parked in my throat.

The confidence in his voice has me blinking back the hot tears.

His thumb brushes over my knuckles. "And Holly?"

"Yeah?" Darkness be damned, my watery voice gives me away.

"When it's not, just know... I see you too."

The room is still, save for the faint creaks of the ancient heater and the soft rhythm of his breathing. The minutes feel stretched thin, like they might snap under the weight of the quiet.

Our final moments before sleep took us filter back in pieces. Chance's hand finding mine in the dark, that quiet "I see you too" that somehow felt bigger than four words should.

Opposite sleeping positions were supposed to make this easier. Less weird.

But the reality? I feel him everywhere.

And everything I feel is so very different from our usual antagonism.

The mattress dips where he lies, his broad frame somehow both too close and impossibly far away.

Even head-to-foot, his presence fills the room, each subtle shift of the bed like a ripple I can't ignore.

Every quiet exhale stirs something restless inside me.

I should close my eyes. Will myself to sleep.

Remember my goal. There's no room for getting distracted by this quietly unguarded version of my brother's best friend—vulnerable in a way I never thought I'd see and impossible to ignore.

But I don't.

Instead, I shift carefully, propping myself up on one elbow.

His shirt rides up slightly, exposing the edge of his lower back, where smooth skin disappears under the waistband of his pants.

I hesitate for a moment before I finally let my fingertips graze the fabric—a tentative touch—and my chest tightens.

Soft and worn from too many washes, it hugs his solid, unyielding strength. Strength you don't get from desk jobs and weekend gym trips.

What am I even looking for? Some sort of proof that this moment isn't as precarious as it feels? Some excuse to let myself keep touching him?

Brushing over his tricep, I soak up the warmth radiating from his skin, my gaze tracing along the taut fabric stretched over defined muscles. I let my fingers linger, skimming just enough to feel the strength beneath the surface, the life I've never been a part of.

Letting my fingers drift lower, I trace the edge of his wrist. The faint ridges of tendon feel like kind of quiet power. He's utterly still, his breathing even and steady, and for one reckless moment, I let my hand settle over his.

His fingers twitch, a small movement that makes my

heart lurch. I freeze, holding my breath as the seconds tick by. But he doesn't wake.

"You're going to make this so much harder, you know that?" I whisper into the quiet. The words are too big for the moment, too raw, but they escape anyway.

He shifts slightly, a soft noise escaping his lips, and I press my palm to my chest like I can keep my heart from beating out of it.

But he doesn't stir further. His breathing evens out again, the steady rhythm a soft comfort I can't explain.

"Is this what it feels like?" I murmur, my voice barely audible even to myself. "To let someone in?"

The words hang in the air, unanswered, as my fingers curl lightly around his. For a long moment, I let the quiet hold us. Let myself trace the edges of a feeling I don't know how to name.

Eventually, I sink back against the pillow, careful not to wake him. My hand lingers a second longer before I pull it away, curling it against my chest like doing so might hold on to the moment.

<h1 style="text-align:center">6
CHANCE</h1>

Jesus fucking Christ.

The first thing my brain registers is warm, soft skin, the intoxicating scent of vanilla, and something uniquely Holly filling my lungs.

Somewhere between our late-night confessions and dawn, I ended up with my face nestled against her inner thigh—my mouth a whisper away from court-martial territory by her brother.

Opening my eyes is a tactical error. A pink flamingo tattoo on her upper thigh peeks out from beneath the hem of my shirt. *Otis*, according to the cursive script beneath its long, elegant neck.

When the hell did Holly get a tattoo? In that ocean of tequila she mentioned last night? And why a flamingo named Otis?

The smug little bird holds a martini glass while

balancing on one leg like he's trying to pass a field sobriety test.

The urge to trace it with my tongue bull-rushes me. Before I can think better of it, my lips part. Military discipline and the bro code crumbles in the face of one tiny pink bird strutting across her skin like he owns the damn place.

Nice and slow, I stretch my neck and settle my mouth over her warm skin.

My lips tingle as I explore a part of her I was never meant to see.

Who the hell is this Holly? The one with named tattoos and fuck-me socks designed to keep a man's cock locked and loaded.

And don't even get me started on the glasses.

Each stolen brush of my lips sends blood surging faster through my veins.

My best friend's annoying little sister somehow made a Ring Pop sexy enough to spark a whole new fetish. One powerful enough to become the top search term on Pornhub.

My eyes sink shut as I fight the urge to dig my fingers into her flesh.

Darting out the tip of my tongue just far enough to get a tortuous taste, I choke back the groan clawing its way up my throat.

The obnoxious little sister who used to relentlessly trail after us with scraped knees has evolved into something far more dangerous.

A woman who embraces her fears and turns them

into bullets of pure determination to take on her father without flinching.

Brave and strong with secret with a perfect balance of tender spots.

Ones I want to discover.

And protect.

Nick never should have been worried about me fucking his little sister… he should have worried about this.

My cock throbs painfully, punishing me for denying him the relief of grinding against her.

Mumbling sleepily, her fingers trail over my hair and settle along the back of my head as she tugs me closer in her sleep.

Heat crawls over my skin. The jagged sound of my choppy breaths pound in my skull.

Her grip tightens, and with unexpected strength, she shoves my head deep between her legs as she sighs, mumbles, and shifts repeatedly on the mattress.

Cotton underwear brush against my nose, a dangerously thin barrier between my promises and the intoxicating warmth I want to get lost in.

A sleep growl of frustration slips from her lips. "Get in there, dammit."

Ummmmm, what?

Another growl rumbles from her this one full of sleepy frustration. Her thighs flex and tighten. Remarkably strong yet delicate fingers lock on to my ears.

S—O—fucking—S.

What started out as quite possibly the single most

erotic wake-up of my life is a fight for survival under the very real threat of suffocation—*fuck.*

"I like it rough as much as the next guy…" The words come out strangled as her legs squeeze tighter. "But maybe we should discuss consent first."

Rambling something unintelligible, she rolls her hips, clearly still deep in whatever dream that has her grinding against my face.

Her scent hits me, heady and undeniable, threading through my senses—a mix of warmth and something that feels like an invitation.

The cotton brushing my nose is damp, teasing me with proof that whatever's happening in her dream has her completely undone.

Holy hell.

My brain scrambles, caught between the heat rolling off her and the way her hips shift in some instinctive, maddening rhythm. It's a wake-up call I'll never forget, one I'm not sure I'd survive twice.

At the first opportunity, I slip from a grip fit for the WWE, but the damage is done.

Her warmth, the soft little sounds she makes—they're burned into my brain like sensitive intel I'll never be able to delete—just like the classified details of her fears, her dreams, and everything she's fighting for.

That Holly, who let her guard down, seems worlds away from the one who's about to wake up.

Rolling onto her back, she flings an arm over her eyes. My shirt parts with her movement, revealing flushed skin and a hint of the curve of her breast that has me reaching for my phone and capturing this glimpse of her.

Just to torment Nick. That's all.

But seeing her like this—relaxed, soft, those damn striped socks still clinging to her thighs like some kind of candy cane fantasy come to life—does something to my chest I'm not ready to examine.

The early morning light catches on her tumbled hair, revealing spun copper strands threaded through the waves.

I focus on her slightly parted lips, bringing me back to how they looked wrapped around her Ring Pop, followed by the soft, sticky sound of it popping free, leaving the wet shimmer of cherry sweetness smeared on her pink, edible—*Mission abort. Mission fucking abort.*

I should delete the photo. My thumb hovers over the trash icon, my chest heaving as two opposing versions of me battle for control.

A better man would delete it, but I can't.

Grasping for normalcy and solid ground, I shoot the image to Nick.

ME

Rise and shine, fucker. Sleep good?

I hope he didn't. If I suffer, he suffers. We go down together. I follow up with every phallic emoji I can think of—a few of them highly questionable. The flashlight looks like a fleshlight and the crossing swords are—whatever, doesn't matter—let him choke on his coffee over that one.

I escape to the safety of the shower before I can analyze my life choices any further. But even scalding water can't wash away the details carving into my memory, rewriting everything I thought I knew about little Holly McAdams.

Twenty minutes later, what should be a normal tooth-brushing routine, is a direct assault on my gums. Frustration fuels my most basic movements… until my eyes lock on a scrap of white cotton panties.

Painted across the back in delicate cursive—"Am I more than you bargained for yet?"—complete with fucking antlers, like some kind of battle cry.

Eyes front. Keep brushing.

And there, right next to this modern declaration of war, a whisper of white lace masquerading as a bra. The two pieces mock me from their perch on the robe hook.

No amount of military discipline could stop me from surrendering to Holly's unintentional act of psychological warfare.

Not exactly the way I planned to go out—from DEFCON five to leveled-by-panties asking the exact question I'm too afraid to answer.

Yeah, Squirt. You're way more than I bargained for.

"Undisclosed fetish I should have known before I shared a bed with you?"

Jumping at the sound of her voice, I choke, setting off a frantic struggle to avoid the dubious honor of being the first person taken down by toothpaste.

She leans against the doorframe, waiting out my struggle, amusement curving her lips.

Meanwhile, despite my possible imminent death, I continue fondling her underwear like some hormone-driven recruit who doesn't know his way around a clit.

And I definitely know my way around a clit.

"Just admiring your, uh, artistic expression." Real smooth, soldier. "Fall Out Boy lyrics? Really?"

"Yes, really. Would you three like to be alone?" She snatches them from my hands, her fingers brushing mine in a way that definitely doesn't make my pulse spike. "They have outpatient services for this sort of thing now."

She's trying for light, but I catch the slight tremor in her voice, the way she won't quite meet my eyes.

Last night changed things, whether we want to admit it or not.

7
Holly

Someone should really invent a system for ranking awkward silences. Like a Richter scale, but for measuring the seismic waves of discomfort radiating between two people trapped in a truck after one catches the other fondling her underwear.

Twenty minutes from the lodge, and my brain keeps replaying the image of Chance in nothing but a towel as he studied my manifestation panties like they held nuclear launch codes.

Well, my systems are activated, and my rockets launched, thankyouverymuch. My girl zone is sparking harder than a live wire. I'm shocked he can't hear the snap, crackle, and pop.

Heat crawls up my neck as I remember the way his fingers traced the cursive script with something close to reverence. Or maybe that was just my hormones reimagining things because, holy body, damn him.

While he studied my underwear, I mapped the mouthwatering contours of corded muscle with intriguing dips and valleys, my fingers itching to touch the entire time.

Look, don't touch, dear.

Cue my mother's voice—the queen of box-blocking.

But touching is so much more fun.

And in this case, about the dumbest thing I could do.

I've seen him in less over the years—weekends at the lake, Fourth of July blowouts where our moms weaponized red, white, and blue, drowning the southeastern shore of Sebago Lake in tacky Americana.

Then came the two-year transformation: from scrawny runt to buff jock, strutting around like Tom Brady showing off his Super Bowl rings.

Told you—GI Jackass isn't just a nickname. It's fifteen years of foreshadowing wrapped in cargo pants and ego.

I steal glances at his profile between frantic taps on my phone, searching for any update on my wayward luggage. His sharp features catch the morning light, all barely contained intensity as he navigates the winding mountain roads. His jaw ticks—that telltale flex that says he's wrestling with something bigger than road conditions. Every twitch of that muscle sends an answering pulse between my thighs.

Jesus, when did that start happening? My body's sudden betrayal is definitely not part of the master plan.

Master plan. Yes. Focus.

"We need to talk." The words pop out of me like a champagne cork—loud, sudden, and with absolutely no chill. Unless, of course, it was chilled.

Oof, I will forever be grateful I didn't let that turd of a joke slip from between my lips. God.

His fingers still on the wheel. "About this morning—"

"No!" Heat floods my cheeks. "Nope. Uh, about my father."

The muscle in his cheek twitches, a dead giveaway, like it's putting on its best national performance, hoping to make the Olympic jaw-flexing team. "What about him?"

Here goes nothing. "I need you to pretend you can't stand me."

He jerks. The truck swerves slightly before he steadies it, his reaction more telling than the neutral "Come again?" that follows.

"When we get there." The words spill out, an avalanche of nerves I can't stop. "I need you to act like I'm still the annoying little sister who drives you nuts. Kick it up a notch, even—who do you have the most disdain for—I'm them."

"Yeah, I'm *not* do—"

"Please." My voice cracks, shrinking into that pathetic little girl who used to trail after him and Nick, desperate to be included. And now, for the pièce de résistance of humiliation. "My father… he hasn't confirmed it, but I have this sinking feeling he's bringing Blake. And he's not exactly subtle about nudging Blake my way every chance—"

"Wait." His voice sharpens. "Blake? The suit Nick said's been sniffing around your dad for the past year?"

"That's the one." My laugh comes out more wheeze than humor. "Pretty sure Dad sees Blake running the company while I play corporate Barbie. But there's no universe, multiverse, or alternate dimension where I'm going blond."

The growl he chokes back sends a shiver down my spine, dangerous and somehow… gratifying. Sunlight catches on his white-knuckled grip on the wheel. "And you're thinking—"

"If my father sees us getting along—because when the hell have we ever gotten along—I know him, he'll latch on to the hope that we're together or something. He'll get it in his head that I'm finally coming around. Getting ready to settle down at some point sooner rather than later."

"With me?" His tone sharpens an edge that makes my skin tingle.

"Not necessarily with you, genius. Just overall." My tone comes out snippier than I intend. "And with someone safe. Someone from the right social circle." I wrinkle my nose at the word. "Which, unfortunately, includes you."

"I'm barely in his social circle and I sure as hell am

not safe." There's that growl again, low and simmering, and my stupid toes curl.

"Not that it matters…" His jaw tightens, and the words come out clipped. "Because you're not with me."

Ouch. Okay then. Curling aborted.

"I'm so glad you made that clear. I was confused for a hot minute. Crisis averted, GI Jackass. Still, I'd rather not fuel any hopeful assumptions on his part."

"So what—you want to pretend nothing's changed?"

My stomach drops as his words hit too close to those quiet moments in the dark. When I let myself trace the edges of his wrist, feeling the quiet strength there. Let my fingers drift over his skin like I had any right to.

Oh God.

He wasn't awake. No way. GI Joe would not have just lain there and let me—nope—sure, his fingers twitched under mine, but that was totally involuntary. Meant nothing. Did not mean he knows I—*what?*

Doesn't matter. He doesn't know. I will not be served with a restraining order. It's all fine.

Changed?

Pshawww, please.

"How has anything changed?" I force a shrug. Not that it matters. Whatever new ground this is between us, it has no place in the week ahead.

Right on cue and ready to ruin my life, the memory of his steady breathing, the warmth of his skin under my fingertips, the way I whispered things into the darkness I never meant for him to hear—it all crowds in, threatening to suffocate me.

Bury it now. Slap a tombstone on it. Move right along.

He flicks a glance in my direction, opens his mouth as though he's going to say something, and instead shakes his head and closes it once again. There's something in his expression that makes my chest tight. Like maybe he knows exactly what I did in those stolen moments when I thought I was safe.

Time to get my man—not *my man*, but this man, panty bandit, or whatever—out of the corner he's trying to march us into. And maybe save myself from finding out just how awake he might have been.

"Nothing *has* changed, soldier boy. Fondling my juju bits does not a commitment make."

"I was not fondling your juju bits. I was fondling yo —never mind."

"Fine, my crotch curtain." This. Humor. Humor is good. Humor is healing. It's not denial at all. Course correction at its finest!

His wince is priceless, like I stepped on his junk with my heel. "Those are two words that never need to be side by side again."

"Undercarriage cozy, better?" I've got so many more where that came from, soldier boy. This is my lane. My arm floaties in the deep end.

And since I've never been able to resist a challenge, I'm in the deep end a lot. I really should take swimming lessons. Slap those right on the list after win the company and not falling for ole GI Joe over here with the big—*er*—guns.

He pinches the bridge of his nose. "And another two."

Two guns at least at last count because—you know what, doesn't matter—I'll just task my overactive brain with adding the guns to the flick files.

"Privates po—"

"You're a menace." He pierces me with a look that probably works on his subordinates. He forgets I've seen him as a grown-ass man in an ugly Christmas onesie.

One that was a size too small. Not that I noticed— *much.* Look, I'm programmed to notice those things, okay? Especially when *those things* practically walk into the room before he does.

And the third gun enters the chat. His third gun's got game.

Keeping my eyes straight ahead—*for reasons*, I raise and waggle my finger. "Baby sister, it's in the job description."

"You're not my baby sister." His voice dives into the deep end of my pool and I'm pretty sure I hear the tell-tale hiss of my floaties deflating.

I'm gonna need soldier boy over here to stop dropping lines like he's serving looks.

"Look, if he passes the company to me, I want it to be on my own merit." I go for the kind of in-your-face confidence I've mastered in the corporate world, but at the moment, my words come out softer. More like the optimistic dreamer I used to be. "Not because he thinks I've found someone who'll make me settle down and behave."

That damn tender underbelly of mine has a big mouth and likes telling all my secrets.

She and I are going to have to have another loyalty talk.

He flashes a quick grin. "Behave? He should've seen you at baggage claim."

The band squeezing my chest eases with one line—one smile.

Just like that—*balance restored.*

"And definitely not because he hopes I've finally learned my place."

"Your place?" He snorts, the edge softening into humor. "Men stopped *placing* women somewhere around the time we lost track of the remote."

"Not men like my father."

The fresh blanket of snow turns into a dazzling carpet of diamonds under the powerful sun. It should be beautiful. Instead, it feels like nature conspiring to spotlight every worry gnawing at my insides.

"Shouldn't be too hard anyway. You and Nick will fuck off up the mountain to some supersecret ceremonious circle jerk like you always do. You guys and your covert traditions. You act like you're the first line of protection for the Infinity Stone."

His eyes cut to mine for a split second, something unreadable flickering in their depths. "Nice mouth, Squirt. Nick can crank his own dick, thanks. Bitter much?"

I roll my eyes, refusing to let him see how much his

words affect me. "Please. I'm way too mature to hold decade-old grudges about being excluded from your sword-swinging boys' brigade." Crossing my arms, I aim for nonchalance. "I outgrew giving a shit a long time ago."

Chance slides me a look, one eyebrow arched. "You sound like it. Must be why you spent that one whole week alone stalking the shit out of us."

Heat rushes to my cheeks. "I was twelve!"

"You were a felon in the making." His lips twitch, fighting a smile.

"Gee, and look at me now. No record." This is where I'd flip my hair for emphasis if I hadn't cut a bunch of it off.

"Yet." He shakes his head, but there's something almost fond in his tone that makes my stomach flutter. "So damn stubborn then. Still are."

His gaze locks with mine, and for a moment, the air between us crackles with an energy I can't quite name. It's like some primal part of me recognizes it and responds to it on a cellular level, hijacking my heart rate all over again.

I swallow hard, trying to ignore the way my pulse pounds in my ears. "It's not like it was a no-girls-allowed sausage fest. That local girl used to hang out with you guys all the time. Sierra something. *She* was allowed to hang with the boys."

"Sierra was different." Chance's thumb taps against the steering wheel, a subtle smile curving his lips. "Besides, maybe some things are worth the wait."

The words hang between us, loaded with a meaning I'm not sure I'm ready to unpack.

Different how? The question claws at the back of my throat, bitter and insistent. Different like a girl who's one of the guys? Different like unforgettable? Or just different because she had the kind of poise and charm that doesn't come with a side of sarcasm and eye rolls?

And what's with the "worth the wait" comment anyway? Who's waiting? Sierra didn't have to wait. It was a *hey there, boys,* and boom, Gold VIP membership holder.

"Careful, GI Joe. So it's not a sword-crossing sausage fest... a bukkake ruins carpets scenario with Sierra in the mix. Got it."

"And here I thought your biggest weapon was sarcasm. Turns out it's shock value. Do you kiss the coffee guy with that mouth or just scare him into free refills?"

"Sure do. Suck the occasional dick with it too. So, nailed it, right? Total bukkake."

A pained expression flickers across his face, and he shifts in his seat. "No carpet to ruin at the Shred Shack, not interested in trading the afterglow on post-bukkake cleanup duty."

He's kidding. He said it all deadpan... definitely kidding—I think. Not that it matters. I just don't want to picture Nick like that. That's all. That's precisely it.

And the Shred Shack? Seriously? Sounds like the brainchild of a dude-bro who skipped leg day.

But this bukkake chick got to go there. Not that he

confirmed it. But he didn't deny it, either—somehow, that's worse.

And it's not like I want to be Sierra. I don't. I don't even want him. This is just… curiosity. Normal, harmless curiosity.

So, different how? Different like perfect? Different like the kind of girl who doesn't make jokes about bukkake in casual conversation?

God, stop. Just stop. It's fine. Totally fine. I don't care what he meant by "worth the wait." I don't.

Except I do. And I hate her for it, whoever she is—or was. Ugh, who even waits for someone anymore?

8

Holly

The circular drive curves past luxury SUVs to the grand entrance of the Morgan Lodge at Ridgewood Peak.

The very place we've spent our Christmases for forever.

Stone pillars frame massive oak doors, and evergreen garlands drape the archway. Fresh powder sparkles on every surface, picture-perfect and serene.

Chance kills the engine but doesn't move. "You sure about this?"

No. Not even a little bit. But I nod anyway.

We grab our bags and head inside, looking less like we're about to hit the slopes and more like we're—oh, I don't know—facing down a firing squad.

"You should smile, you look like you're headed for a

colonoscopy." I aim for a teasing tone, but it comes out harsher than I intended.

"You think smiling will fix that?" His voice is sharp and mocking at the very suggestion.

"Don't know. I just know that's what you guys tell us. Like it's the goddamn answer to world peace or some shit." The words taste bitter on my tongue after a lifetime of being told every problem could be solved if I just beamed like a little ray of toxic sunshine while I rode a unicorn farting rainbows.

Chance's brow furrows. "Does your dad emit some vibe that dials you straight to some 'fuck all the way off' setting or something?"

No.

Well.

Maybe.

Probably.

Yes, okay. The answer is yes. How uncouth of him to point it out.

I flip him the bird—complete with my tongue out. Gotta get in character and all that. Apparently, diapers are in order if my souring mood is any indication.

"Charming."

We cross the lobby, the scent of pine and cinnamon drifting through the air. It should be comforting, but the knot in my stomach only tightens.

As we approach the archway leading to the great room, I slow.

"Remember—"

"I know, I know. Pretend to hate your guts. Got it," he mutters, his voice tight.

Before I can say more, the synchronized squeals of the Sentimental Squad—otherwise known as our mothers—pierce the air.

"I've seen this before," I whisper, nodding toward the room full of holiday cheer and family drama waiting for us. "*The Last of Us*, episode five?"

"A horde of fungus zombies. Yup. Didn't they use Molotov cocktails? Because I'm fresh out."

"What a tragic misuse of overly tactical cargo pants," I smirk, letting my gaze drift to his legs—an immediate mistake. This pair is somehow even tighter than the last.

"Chance! You made it!" His mother's voice is shrill with delight, her designer boots clicking rapidly across the polished hardwood floor as she rushes toward us.

Mrs. McAllister swoops in, enveloping Chance in a hug so fierce it practically redefines parental guilt trips. The kind of hug that screams, *I missed you so much, how dare you leave me alone with your father for this long.*

Right on cue, my mom, hovering like a caffeinated hummingbird, wraps her arms around me, pulling me into a warm, perfumed embrace that somehow manages to both comfort and smother me at the same time. "You look too thin. Have you been eating? Are you taking vitamins?"

Charlie breaks away from where she's wrapped around Nick to shoot me a knowing look that makes my cheeks flame.

Eve—the family chaos engine—has that hawkeyed, forensic glare of hers primed and pinned on us. Nothing's slipping past her radar. I don't know whether to cheer her on or start building a bunker. She's the perfect storm of brilliant and devious—a real asset when the wheels come off until she's the one lighting the fuse.

Charlie better keep her mouth shut—she knows precisely which skeletons I've got stashed, and I'm not in the mood for a surprise exorcism.

"Oh, look at that!" Mrs. McAdams gasps, pointing skyward like she's just uncovered the lost city of Atlantis. "Mistletoe!"

Frozen to the spot, a buzz vibrates to the roots of my hair, leaving a trail of goosebumps behind.

Chance stiffens beside me, every muscle taut like he's preparing for battle.

And really, he should be. Because, of course, there's mistletoe. Why wouldn't there be mistletoe?

The universe clearly decided I needed one last kick while I'm down. And naturally, Chance had to be so freakishly tall, forcing his mom to crane her neck and spot that little sprig overhead.

Taking a strategic step back, he flashes a tight smile full of forced cheer. "I'm good."

His tone is so perfectly casual it's almost suspicious. Like he's rehearsed sounding indifferent just for moments like this.

"It's bad luck to ignore tradition," she adds, throwing me so far under the bus I can practically feel the tire treads on my back.

Charlie's eyes gleam. My brain kicks into overdrive, trying to calculate just how many gift-wrapped grenades I've handed her in text by mentioning Chance.

And Nick? Oh, Nick isn't even pretending to play it cool. His focus is laser-locked on Chance, his shoulders tense, jaw tight, and his mouth forming a grim line daring Chance—*Try it, bro. I dare you. Just give me a reason to deck your fucking halls.*

This is my nightmare.

Ho. Ho. Ho.

This is stupid. It's mistletoe. And like they say about *doth protesting too much* or something like that. Look, I'm better with numbers.

Point is, the longer we stand here, the bigger the deal it is.

Screw it.

Curling my fingers in the front of his shirt—firm grip on both dog tags if you know what I mean—I yank him down.

Rising onto my toes, I press a hard, decisive kiss to his mouth.

There's no hesitation, no softness—just bold, take-no-prisoners action to shut everyone up and get it over with.

Only… his lips are soft. Warm. They part slightly in surprise, and something electric zips through me, making more than my toes curl.

My nipples all of a sudden dress up like Mr. Peanut, complete with top hat and cane doing a Broadway number worthy of a Tony Award.

His hand grips my hip, firm and steady—whether to keep me balanced or to keep me there, I can't tell. My pulse stutters. A whimper pounds its little fist in my throat, demanding to be set free. Before I go from zero to screwing the proverbial pooch less than five minutes into my grand plan, I jerk back.

The rest of our families surge forward with hugs and greetings, but their voices barely register. They're blissfully normal, passing us around for the obligatory forced affection like the world didn't just tip on its axis.

My lips tingle where his mouth touched mine, every nerve ending alive and buzzing with dangerous awareness.

"Holly!" My dad's booming voice slices through the chaos, jolting me out of my haze.

My eyes snap up to the direction of his voice and—*called it!*

"There's someone who can't wait to see you!"

Can't wait, my ass.

Blake stands at my father's side in an impeccably tailored suit that probably costs more than my monthly rent. His smug smile has me fantasizing about wiping it off with a well-placed elbow.

"You remember Blake." He claps Blake on the back, beaming with the kind of pride I can only dream of earning—pride currently wasted on this walking Ralph Lauren ad with the personality of a doorknob.

"This young man is single-handedly responsible for breaking the record for new accounts in a single year."

Translation: *Look how perfect he'd be running my company while you play the dutiful wife.*

I paste on a saccharine smile. "How could I forget? Though I hear it's not the number of accounts that matters—it's the profit they bring in."

Blake's smirk doesn't falter, like I didn't just insult his... performance. "You're looking lovely as ever, Holly. I hope we can catch up later."

I'd rather have one of Charlie's "toys" stuck in Tab C and spend the night explaining my life choices to a hot proctologist, thanks.

I cock my head, my smile sharpening like lethal icicles I picture driving through his eye. "Oh, I'm sure we'll have plenty of time to... compare numbers."

Beside me, Chance coughs into his fist, poorly concealing a laugh.

Blake's eyes narrow.

"Don't get the kids started, William. No work at Christmas. That's the rule. You can talk numbers at home."

Blech—I will never be talking about my father's numbers in any capacity ever, Mom, but you do you.

Mom gives my father a pointed look and presses a room key into my palm. "Your room key, dear. Though I'm sure you'll spend more time on the slopes than in it."

More like buried in spreadsheets, but she doesn't need to know that.

Dad waits until my Mom's attention is firmly fixed on greeting Chance before his hand settles on my shoulder, the affectionate squeeze making his habit of repeatedly dismissing me cut all the deeper.

I love him, but I don't really like him.

I miss being the kid who didn't know better, who could just love him in blissful ignorance. Way back when loving him didn't hurt.

"Join Blake and me in the library soon, would you? We'd love your input on some projections."

Because apparently, I'm good enough to play the role of the pretty little think tank—here to make their proposals shine before being shuffled off to the sidelines.

Fiery irritation burns under my skin. Let them underestimate me. It's almost adorable how little they know about what I've got in my arsenal—a pitch sharp enough to draw blood and the guts to use it.

I risk one last glance at Chance, and I hear his quiet words once again.

I see you too.

Under the intensity of his stare, my frustration morphs into determination.

Suddenly, I can't wait to show them all exactly how big I can dream.

<h1 style="text-align:center">9
CHANCE</h1>

Her taste lingers on my lips like an unauthorized security breach.

Sweet.

Dangerous.

The kind of chaos that turns the strongest of men into fools.

And let's be honest—I deserve it. I've spent the past year giving Nick endless grief about Charlie. Now, here I am, a walking cliché, fighting my dozenth hard-on just being in close proximity.

You know, like the same zip code.

I watch her walk away, trying like hell not to notice how that skirt hugs every curve.

Or how she still has that little swing in her step—the one that used to drive us nuts when we were kids because it meant she was up to something.

Only now it's driving me nuts for entirely different reasons.

I suck in a breath. The familiar scent of pine and cinnamon fills my lungs, dragging me back to a childhood that refuses to let go.

Same massive stone fireplace where Holly set the stockings on fire trying to roast marshmallows when she was eight—still scarred from her attempt at "campfire chic."

Same worn leather armchairs where Nick and I plotted every harebrained scheme while she sat behind books, pretending not to eavesdrop.

Same Holly who tagged along after us, all scraped knees and pure, unrelenting determination.

Different Holly—one who kisses like she's declaring war and laughs like she's already won it.

"You coming?" Nick's voice cuts through my definitely-not-appropriate thoughts about his sister.

"Yeah." I scrub a hand over my face. Between the drive, the night at the hotel with Holly, and that kiss—I'm running on fumes.

Horny, lust-filled fumes. "You owe me a drink."

Or ten.

Preferably ones strong enough to drown out everything your sister did to me in the last twelve hours.

Between her early morning exploration of my face and the way she trusted me with her fears, sleep feels impossible. Every time I close my eyes, I feel her fingertips ghosting over my skin.

And if I don't lock it up, my best friend is going to see it written all over my face.

Survival skills engaged.

Fifteen minutes later, I'm leaning on the bar, burning up every last bit of energy trying to look like the picture of nonchalance while Nick makes it his mission to set me on fire with his piercing glare.

It's all about who can hold out under the cloud of silent judgment the longest. Something we both excel at considering our families, but his loud as fuck silence is ruining our Pappy's tradition.

"For fuck's sake, stop looking at me like that." I down half my drink in one go, savoring the burn. "Your face might stick that way and when my sister kicks your ass to the curb, then what will you do?"

"Nice deflection." Nick's eyes narrow. "You want to explain that photo you sent me this morning?"

"Which one? The eggplant emoji parade or—"

"You know damn well which one." He sets his drink down with more force than necessary. "The one of my sister looking thoroughly debauched in your shirt."

My mind flashes to Holly in my flannel, all soft curves and sleepy eyes.

Yup, not helping the boner status one fucking bit.

"Debauched?" I snort. "Next thing you're going to accuse me of is knowing the color of her knickers."

I happen to know, but let's not split hairs.

"Deflecting. Again."

Goddamn right I am.

I'm hoping to hold out to the second Pappy's.

Drown my bone in a little ninety proof because it's impolite to point. Especially when it's at your best friend —mid interrogation.

Just call me Mr. Goddamn Manners.

He jams a hand through his hair, and I remember doing the same a few hundred times when he and Charlie played out through text while I was half a world away.

"Just tell me you didn't sleep with her."

The weight of her secrets sits heavy in my chest.

Holly tracing my features in the dark.

Holly whispering her fears to my supposedly sleeping form.

The trust in those moments means more than any physical contact could.

No, Nick… I didn't fuck your sister. But with her every lingering touch in the dark when she thought I was sleeping… she fucked me. Really fucked me.

Didn't sleep with her.

"You saw the picture, the room only had one bed." Okay, low blow, but I'm not ready to have this conversation. Not after spending half the night keeping myself awake so I could hold her hand longer.

"Answer the fucking question, McAllister."

Every cell goes still at his tone. Thirty years of friendship with Nick sitting like lead in my gut.

"Do you see stretch marks around her lips?"

I take way too much pleasure in the way his mouth goes slack.

"Is she walking funny?"

And now hangs open.

"No?" The tension between us pulses as I hold his stare. "Then I guess I didn't fuck your sister."

Oblivious to the self-loathing in my voice, his shoulders relax slightly.

"The way you two were looking at each other under that mistletoe…"

"That was all your mother's doing." Which is true enough.

The kiss itself, though?

All Holly—sweet, spicy, no longer struggling to keep up, but instead charging ahead.

"It was a joke, man." The ice in my glass clinks as I swirl the amber liquid. "You left me with Squirt duty. I was simply keeping you updated on the mission status."

"With visual aids?"

"I'm thorough like that."

"Yeah?" He leans forward. "How about you be thorough explaining why you looked ready to commit murder when Blake showed up?"

Shit. He caught that?

"Professional courtesy. Guy's a douche."

"So you're what—going to stare daggers at every guy who looks at my sister?"

"If necessary." I flash him a grin. "Think of me as your eyes on the ground."

"Well shit, look what the storm dragged in!" A familiar voice booms across the bar.

Everett Morgan's grin is exactly as I remember it— wide and genuine, with just a hint of trouble brewing underneath. Time's been good to him. He carries himself with the easy confidence of a man who knows his place in the world.

"Morgan." I stand, accepting his bear hug with a laugh. "Still terrorizing the slopes?"

"Someone's gotta keep you city boys humble." He drops into the seat next to me, signaling the bartender. "Though I hear you're not exactly living the soft life these days. How many deployments now?"

"Seven." I take another sip of whiskey. "Just there for intelligence purposes. Less glamorous than it sounds."

"Unless you count all the penetration," Nick mutters with a grin into his glass.

I shoot him a look promising retribution.

"How's the lodge treating you?"

"Same shit, different snow." Everett's eyes scan the room, then stop.

His whole body goes still.

"Well, hello gorgeous. Please tell me she's not with either of you because that—" He lets out a low whistle. "Is worth breaking my 'no guests' rule for."

My gut clenches as I follow his gaze. Holly stands near the fireplace, all bare legs and flushed cheeks, with her head thrown back in laughter at something Charlie just said.

One sweeping perusal of her elegant throat and my mouth runs dry.

The same throat I wanted to taste this morning.

Fuck.

"Pipe down, hotshot. That's my sister," Nick says flatly.

"No way." Everett's eyes widen. "Little Holly?" He lets out another whistle. "Damn. Time has been very, very kind."

A growl builds in my chest. "Watch it."

Nick and Everett's heads turn to me in tandem.

Shit.

"Something you want to share?" Nick's voice carries that edge again.

"Just looking out for your sister." I force a casual shrug. "Like I said—eyes on the ground."

"Speaking of looking out for her—" Everett grins, clearly enjoying the tension. "Remember that time Holly tried to find our clubhouse? Made it halfway up the back trail before you two noticed she was following you?"

The memory hits and the whiskey turns rancid on my tongue. Holly, maybe twelve, determination written all over her face as she tried to keep up. Snow clinging to her red mittens, eyes bright with hope until we crushed it.

God, we were such assholes.

"She got her revenge, though." Nick chuckles. "What was it—salt in our canteens?"

"Ghost peppers," I correct, phantom heat burning my tongue. "And that was just the beginning."

The taste burned into my memory alone makes me reach for my water. "We probably deserved worse."

"Probably?" Nick snorts. "We definitely deserved worse. She cried for days after that."

My chest tightens. "Yeah, well, we were idiots."

"Were?" Everett smirks.

My phone buzzes with a text from my contact at the airport—Holly's luggage is en route with a buddy of mine. At least something's going right today.

"Rest up—" Everett's grin turns wicked. "Mistletoe can be a demanding bitch."

"She can demand all she wants, it's not happening." I toss some bills on the bar. "Once was enough."

"Sure it was." Nick's tone carries enough bite to strip paint.

I flip them both off without looking back, but Everett's laughter follows me out.

One look at my room key tells me they got us in their family wing. Basically a cluster of rooms all in the same hallway. I get the sentiment, but fuck, there really is no escape.

The main lodge empties out, most guests getting in their last runs before the sun goes down, taking with it about twenty degrees.

Holly's dad and his twenty-four seven ass-kisser bragged about a dinner meeting in town earlier, effectively killing our tradition of having a big family dinner we usually have the first night.

Works for me.

The silence in my room, one I've stayed in many times before, is only broken by the soft whisper of snow against the window.

The bed's exactly where it was twenty years ago when Nick and I used to sneak down to raid the kitchen after lights out.

Holly caught us most of the time, naming the price of her silence. The bargain basement price of bringing her back a cookie.

We always did. Even when we were being assholes about everything else, we couldn't resist that face.

Just like I couldn't resist her kiss today.

My phone buzzes, thank fuck, yanking me from the memory.

Of the kiss, not the cost of her bribes.

HOLLY

Guess what just arrived?

HOLLY

My luggage, you sneaky bastard.

HOLLY

How did you manage that?

I grin at my phone, picturing her excited face.

ME

I know people.

ME

Got everything you need?

HOLLY

All my presentation materials safe and sound.

HOLLY

My laptop's running like a drunk snail
though.

HOLLY

And I share a wall with Blake so
that's fun.

The growl is out before I can stop it.

ME

Everything okay? Want to switch?

HOLLY

Define okay...

HOLLY

He's knocked twice already.

HOLLY

Are conjugal visits a thing in prison?
Asking for a friend who might murder
him if he tries again.

Red bleeds into the edges of my vision. The urge to
knock on his door myself is almost overwhelming.

ME

Need backup?

HOLLY

Nope. I'm good.

HOLLY

But seriously... thank you. For the
luggage rescue.

HOLLY

And for checking on me.

The tightness in my chest eases at her words.

This is the Holly I remember—the one who notices the little things. Who fights like hell but is always thankful for kindness.

The one I'm definitely going to hell for wanting.

ME

Always.

ME

Hey, Squirt...

HOLLY

Yeah, Jackass?

There it is. That spark of humor that's so Holly.

Impressive how she wields sarcasm even when she's imploding inside. A smile tugs at my mouth. She's tough, always finding a way to pull herself back from the edge, even when the ground is shifting under her feet.

ME

This is your presentation to lose. Don't let your father get in your head. He doesn't deserve that power. You're the only one who can give it to him.

Dots appear, doing the digital wave over and over, only to disappear thirty seconds later. Each one ticking away is a reminder that I'm way too invested in this.

No reply.

They flash on the screen again. Stop. Then reappear.

I can't help but watch the hypnotic little bastards like

they might hold the answer to the age-old question: which came first, the chicken or the goddamn egg, while the Jeopardy theme song plays through my head: do-do-do-do, do-do-do…

Pure. Fucking. Agony. My lungs squeeze tight as she keeps me suspended somewhere between anticipation and the urge to throw my phone across the room.

> HOLLY
>
> **Get some sleep, soldier boy.**

I blink down at her response, the relief so powerful, I'm dizzy from it.

> HOLLY
>
> **Fresh battle tomorrow.**

She has no idea. But that's tomorrow's problem.

Tonight, I map out the lodge's entrances and exits in my head, calculating alternate routes that avoid that damn entryway and its mistletoe entirely.

Mission parameters set.

No more mistletoe incidents. No more kisses. No more testing my control.

I'm a soldier. I can follow simple orders.

Even if I know the war is already lost.

Nothing screams 'tis the season for existential dread quite like a family brunch at the lodge. The mimosas are mercifully strong—bless the gods of overpriced orange juice—but I swear the fireplace is in on the joke. Every crackle and pop of the logs sounds like a cackle. As if the fireplace is gleefully rubbing its sooty hands together, awaiting the implosion.

Well, not today. Nope, today I'm the picture of calm, buzzed on spiked champagne, with just enough clarity to watch our parents and ask—*what the fuck?*

"Remember the scavenger hunts?" My mom's voice drips nostalgia. "The kids spent hours running through the lodge…"

"Gingerbread house competitions were my favorite." Chance's mom sighs. "Until the hot glue gun incident—"

"It was one time," Charlie interjects. "His eyebrow grew back eventually. Let it go."

Nick rubs the aforementioned eyebrow. "Eventually is the operative word."

The dining room radiates perfection, from the polished wood beams to the antique sideboards.

Martha Stewart cheer meets rustic luxury.

I take another sip of my mimosa. I've got a lovely little zing to maintain.

"Mom, we've outgrown this," I say, minus the instinctive whine I would have used as a kid. "You can't force us back into our footie pajamas with a sentimental trip down memory lane and hot chocolate."

Mrs. McAllister sweeps a pointed look over all of us. "Well, this is all we've got until one of you finally gives us grandchildren."

"Shots fired," I mutter, earning a sharp look from my mother.

Nick looks at me and jerks his head toward our moms—*You want to help us here?*

"Don't look at me. You and Charlie are the ones trying to make breeding an Olympic sport."

"Holly!" My mother gasps.

I wiggle my glass in the air and shrug. "Weren't you the one who ordered the alcohol?"

"Maybe we could resurrect some of the old traditions. Gingerbread fondue parties at midnight, the snowshoe race…

And those trips to the ER…

"Oh, and the sleigh ride…"

"With the stars overhead, the blankets, the hot chocolate—"

And Nick in the back row of said sleigh finger banging some redhead right up against the pile of gifts for all the good little boys and girls.

Yes. Magical. The very embodiment of the Christmas spirit. Ho-fucking-ho-fucking-ho.

"Are you *trying* to guarantee we avoid all being here at the same time again for the next decade?" Eve asks.

The ensuing back and forth fades away with another sip of my emotional support cocktail.

My father holds court at the head of the table, all margins and projections, oblivious to the child abuse by our mothers shoving us into a candy-coated hellscape.

Wildly different topics of discussion unfold all at once, with everyone taking part.

Except Blake. Because fuck that guy.

We're *Phantom of the Opera* without the chandelier crash—dramatic and polished—ignoring the cracks just beneath the surface.

"The market's primed for aggressive growth," he announces to Chance's father. "Particularly in emerging tech sectors—"

"Actually," I murmur into my mimosa, "tech's showing signs of correction. Third quarter earnings were down twelve percent across the board and haven't rebounded in the fourth quarter."

He doesn't even pause. "And with the right positioning—"

Am I really supposed to let the opportunity that wording provides slide?

Fiiiinnnnnneeee.

I better get points for that, Santa, you jolly bastard you.

"Supply chain disruptions in Asia indicate further volatility," I add, keeping my tone light, my answer PG.

See, I'm a good girl. Send me a big dick. Make him pretty. Bonus points if he's silent.

Chance presses his leg against mine.

You work quick, Santa. I should have been more specific, though. A man with a big dick, not a big dick of the walking variety. He is pretty. And silent. I'll give you that. Two out of three ain't bad, but what's your return policy?

"Healthcare's the real opportunity," Blake chimes in, clearly trying to impress. "Particularly biotech startups—"

"Regulatory hurdles are increasing," I say to no one in particular. "But hey, if you want to sell your soul—"

"Precisely why timing is crucial," my father continues like I'm not even here.

Nick's expression softens across the table. "Holly—"

"It's fine. Really." I wave him off with a genuine smile. And surprisingly, it is. Thanks to a few late-night words from Chance.

My father is just like one of those old See 'n Say toys —pull the string, get the same predictable response.

I didn't have to yank that many times before Nick noticed.

It's something.

I'll take it as a win.

And with that, I'm clinging to Chance's words with the same gusto with which he coveted my peach pouch.

Besides, Chance did say this week was about skiing, booze, and bad decisions.

He definitely was onto something with the drinking.

Soak the dysfunction in a little bit of bubbly. Let chill overnight. Pair with puffed pastries and fresh berries. Problem solved.

Gaze sweeping over our parents one by one, I'm struck by how different they are than us. They live the norms with an effortless ease, like they were made for it —or worse, like they like it there, cocooned in the imbalance of power. Comfortable in the hierarchy, where inequality isn't a flaw but the natural order of things.

Are they really just thirty years older than us? Because with the mimosa goggles on, the generation gap is less of a gap and more of the goddamn Grand Canyon on steroids. *How did these people ever go from posh refinement to bumping uglies?*

There is no way our dads got anywhere near our mothers' slot C's.

Whatdya wanna bet?

They all went to college, but fuck if I could imagine any of them playing beer pong or pounding shots.

Mmmmm, shots. Dancing. Dancing on tables. Man, they missed out.

I slap my palms on the table, give it a couple of jerks —*not that kind*—and test it for durability.

Good ol' timeless stability... check.

Could double as a dance floor in a pinch… check.

Wonder what it would look like holding a buffet of Jell-O shots. Move over gingerbread and carols, yours truly is calling for spiked eggnog and wrecking the halls!

Wooooowwwwwww.

Switching to coffee now.

"Problem?" Chance's clipped tone slices through the general breakfast chaos.

"Not at—*Hic.*"

Whoops.

Smooth.

Very dignified.

"Uh-huh." He raises an eyebrow. His deadpan delivery lands like a sucker punch, and I'm the sucker.

"It's fine. I'm totally fine." Firmly on my way to better than fine once I find my dignity.

Slippery little bitch has to be around here somewhere.

Hic.

"Then do you think you could pass the syrup?"

"Of course, but first, what do you say?"

His gaze swings to mine, one eyebrow pitched in smug, smart-ass form "Now."

"Dick."

"You have no idea, Squirt." He snorts out a laugh that should have the appeal of the ol' lady cave during a sandstorm but, somehow, is charming.

The boob.

With a solid shove, I send the syrup gliding down the

table, the pitcher coming to a perfect stop right in front of him. Not too drunk to operate syrup. Sweet. But still… Coffee? Where the hell is that carafe?

"Anything else, Your Highness?"

The coffee sits just out of reach, but I'm sure as hell unwilling to ask him to pass it. Shoving to my feet, I reach across GI Jackass while he douses his pancakes in an obscene amount of maple syrup.

"That'll do, peasant."

Peasant. *Peasant?*

Before I can stop myself—well, not true, I could have stopped myself, I just didn't feel like it—I give him a slow, theatrical once-over.

"Peasant? Are you under the impression this is a monarchy? Must be hard ruling a kingdom when your biggest"—I shoot a pointed glare at his lap—"*asset* is how much stuff you can cram into sixteen pockets."

Chance's fork freezes halfway to his mouth.

Direct. Fucking. Hit.

That's right, bitches!

With my verbal carnage delivered, I pivot dramatically—as dramatically as one can when the room's leaning a little to the left—grab my waffle, and cram a massive bite into my mouth.

I ignore my mother's glare and focus on the crisp, buttery perfection exploding in my mouth. Syrup drizzled with finesse. The total opposite of soldier boy's—

"Kitten," Blake's voice slides greasily across the table. "Would you pass the butter?"

Freezing mid-chew, I barely manage to suppress a snarl.

A spoon clatters to a plate. Whose, I don't know.

Charlie's head snaps up.

Even Eve's pierced eyebrow arches with predatory interest.

Our fathers still prattle on like his corporate dingleberry didn't just march into battle armed with nothing but a pair of knockoff superhero underoos and a helmet with a lower protection rating than a foil hat.

"Pass the butter?" A shiver of disgust crawls down my spine. I fix him with a flat stare, his words obliterating my buzz with the precision of catching your parents mid-grind.

"Sure. Want me to butter your toast while I'm at it, or do you think you can manage that one on your own, *champ*?"

Champ ends on a satisfyingly distinct pop, making his jaw tick and the vein in his temple throb.

Jokes on you, Bitch Boy. It's sexy when Chance does it.

Not that I noticed.

"Princess," he tries again, "perhaps you'd like to—"

"Listen here, murder muffin." I lean forward, stabbing another bite of waffle. "Unless the next words out of your mouth are 'I'm leaving,' shut it."

Nick chokes on his coffee.

Our dads fall silent, darting looks between us like they've been frolicking through a Mary Poppins daydream, only to realize they've wandered straight into a war zone.

"Sooooo, Holly," Mrs. McAllister chirps, "remember those winter formal dances we used to host here? You girls would spend hours getting ready—"

Smooth transition you got there, Dick's mom. Real smooth.

"And the boys would spend hours avoiding it," Charlie adds with a forced laugh.

"Until Sierra talked them into it," my mother adds with a knowing smile.

The temperature in the room drops ten degrees, or maybe that's the rest of my buzz packing its bags for the fucking Bahamas.

As if summoned by her name alone, a tall blonde appears in the doorway, looking like she just stepped out of a winter wonderland photo shoot.

Because of course she does.

"Has anyone seen Everett?" Sierra's voice carries that hint of cultured polish that makes my skin itch.

Must be clinical. Airborne. Contagious.

Save yourselves, boys.

"That man is impossible to track down when he's—" She stops short, her perfect lips forming a perfect *O* of surprise. "Nick! Chance!"

Her cheeks flush pink—not the blotchy kind like mine, but the kind that probably comes with its own Instagram filter.

She's distracted, clearly annoyed about something, but still manages to look like a Nordic Christmas card come to life—rosy, ethereal, and so damn perfectly composed.

"Little Sierra Barrett!" Mrs. McAllister practically levitates with delight. "Look at you, just as lovely as ever. Join us!"

"Oh, I couldn't, I—" Her gaze drifts to Chance. "I really need to find Everett. His joke of a grant application… for the renovation—you know—never mind."

My stomach clenches.

Renovation?

So she's not just here to look pretty in ski pants for the day.

She'll be around.

Super.

"Such a shame." Chance's mother sighs. "You know, dear." She leans in and winks. "Chance has a thing for blondes."

I definitely don't think about how that applies to me.

Or how it doesn't.

Or why I care.

Not at all.

I picked a hell of a time to quit drinking. You know, five minutes ago.

Look—the first step is admitting you have a problem. I've got ninety-nine but dragging my father's legacy out of the stone age ain't one.

Today anyway.

Statuesque Nordic chick on the other hand…

"Mom," Chance says with a tone that tells her to shutty, without telling her to shutty.

I need him to teach me that.

"Okay, that's enough alcohol for you," Eve says as she swipes the partial mimosa from Mrs. McAllister's hands. "Jesus, Mom, a little tact."

"Don't 'Jesus, Mom' me, young lady. I'm the one who taught manners in the first place. Every lesson—"

"Was built on the foundation of 'Do as I say, not as I do.' Come on, take a walk with me."

"Not that his taste for blondes worked out so well with Noelle," Mr. McAllister adds dryly, watching Eve disappear out the doorway with his wife.

Chance goes deathly still next to me, his fork crashing onto his plate. The room fills with a charged silence.

"Who's Noelle?" The words are out before I can stop them.

"Ancient history," Nick says quickly, his tone warning.

"A mistake," Charlie adds, shooting a glare at Chance's dad.

Silent and unflinching, Chance's gaze drills into his father with a burning intensity no amount of manifestation panties or mimosas combined could give me the nerve to deliver.

"His ex-wife," Mr. McAllister finishes, giving Chance a look almost as cutting back.

Ex-wife.

My stomach bottoms out, the mimosas roiling. But worse than that is the betrayal. He had a wife and I'm the only one who doesn't know?

After I let him in and he held my hand? After trusting him with parts of myself I've never shown anyone—he couldn't trust me with this?

I don't miss the way Chance snatches his knee from where he had purposely pressed it against mine.

Not that I care.

It's not like it was in the job description or anything.

Just like I definitely don't care that his type is apparently blond and different and probably doesn't make bukkake jokes at breakfast.

Probably doesn't lie awake at night like a lovesick idiot, mapping his face with trembling fingers, either.

Sierra shifts uncomfortably in the doorway. "I should really go find—"

"We should do something!" my mother chirps, either oblivious to or deliberately ignoring the tension. "Let's start with that sleigh ride. Tonight, perhaps?"

"Can't," Charlie says quickly. "Nick and I have plans."

All eyes turn to me.

"Oh no." I hold up my hands. "I went looking for a man in finance, trust fund, six-five, blue eyes, and only found spreadsheets."

What the hell am I saying?

"The kind of project your mother warns you against falling for."

My. Fucking. God.

"Thanks to Taylor Swift, I can fix him. No, really, I can."

Kill me now. I just blurted that word salad in front of the Bombshell Bukakke Queen.

Forget that return request, Santa. You're probably just going to repossess.

My mother turns hopeful eyes on Chance while I try not to die on the spot. "Surely you're free?"

Surely he's free?

Woman! Do you not see that he's Hulking the fuck out here???

Technically, he's free for now.

Give him an hour, and he might be facing the death penalty.

The weight of his silence speaks volumes. He hasn't said a word since his father dropped the Noelle bomb, and I hate that I notice.

Hate that I care.

Because I told him some seriously private shit, and he told me not one fucking thing.

If his text of encouragement were painted on my panties, I'd set them on fire and roast marshmallows.

"Actually," Sierra pipes up, still hovering in the door-way, "If you're free later, Chance, I could use your expertise on some security upgrades Everett is trying to push through for the lodge." Her mouth pinches with irritation. "Maybe you can suggest a better way that's less destructive."

On her, irritation looks charming.

On me, I look like I'm one step away from leveling a tall building.

Something hot and unwelcome curls in my stomach. I refuse to call it jealousy because that would be ridiculous. This is Chance. GI Jackass. The bane of my child-hood existence.

The man who held my hand in the dark when I trusted him with my secret, when I trusted him with my fears and dreams and—No.

Not going there.

"I'm going to hit the slopes before those spreadsheets hit me up for some quality time," I announce, pushing back from the table. "Black diamonds to slay. Numbers to crunch. Empires to build. Voodoo dolls to drive nails into."

As I pass Sierra in the doorway, I definitely don't notice how her height puts her at perfect eye level with Chance.

Or how her blond hair catches the morning light.

Or how she probably knows all about his marriage because apparently, they're still friends if she is comfortable asking for his help—with security, maybe changing her oil, diddling her bean—whatever.

I definitely don't care about any of that.

Just like I definitely don't care that Chance's gaze follows me out of the room.

Or that when I glance back, Sierra's already sliding into my vacated seat.

None of it matters.

I've got work to do and a point to prove.

Let them have their traditions and their perfect blondes and their secret ex-wives.

I've got bigger plans.

Even if my chest aches in a way that has nothing to

do with professional ambition, and everything to do with the man who's apparently been married and divorced without me even knowing.

The man whose knee pressed against mine like a promise. Until he snatched it back.

The man who's probably about to reconnect with Sierra over "security upgrades."

II
CHANCE

The snow crunches under my skis, every glide pounding the same thought into my skull: *I can't outrun this.*

No matter how fast—how far—I'll never escape the single biggest screwup of my life.

Six months of marriage.

Six months of pretending to be someone I'm not.

A lifetime of regret neatly gift-wrapped in shame.

I grip my poles tighter, trying to ground myself in the bite of cold metal against my palms.

The line to the top of the mountain shuffles forward. A steady drip-drip-drip from the lift frame overhead beats down on me as we work our way through. Each icy drop landing on my face and neck another little "fuck you" from the universe.

My shoulders bunch, muscles coiled tight enough to snap.

"Man, your dad zinged you good," Nick says, eyeing me warily.

Yup, that was the other "fuck you" of the day.

Thanks for reminding me, fucker.

My father's words echo in my head, his dead-eyed stare burning through me all over again. The cold bites, but it's got nothing on the glacier that's been parked in my chest since brunch. Each breath feels like swallowing shards of ice.

"Not now," I snap, my jaw clenched so tight it aches.

Tension radiates down my neck, digging between my shoulder blades like claws.

My pulse pounds in my temples, a steady drumbeat of shame and anger.

I couldn't see Holly's face when my father dropped that bomb, but I didn't need to. The way she froze beside me, that catch in her breath, how she shifted away—I haven't stopped feeling it since.

I hurt her, and I can't undo it. The knowledge sits like acid in my gut.

Just gnawing away.

A snowball streaks past my face, followed by high-pitched squealing of a couple of kids locked in mortal combat—snowball style.

"Hey!" I bark, my voice carrying that drill sergeant edge that usually has recruits snapping to attention. My hands curl into fists, knuckles cracking. "Take it somewhere else."

They ignore me completely.

Fucking great.

A muscle ticks in my jaw.

Another projectile flies by, spraying ice crystals across my face. My fingernails bite into my palms.

Deep breaths.

They're just kids.

"Might want to dial it back there, Captain America." Charlie's voice floats over my shoulder. "Your murder face is showing."

"Pretty sure that's his regular face today," Eve adds.

Great. Just who I need crawling up my ass right now.

Only I turn to find not just Charlie and Eve, but Holly too. The sister trifecta, come to witness my rapid unraveling.

My heart slams against my ribs.

Holly's studying the snow like it holds the secrets to corporate domination.

Avoiding my gaze.

And from the looks of it, stone-cold sober.

The flush on her cheeks isn't from champagne this time—it's from the cold. Or anger. Probably both.

My father has that effect on people. The bastard's always known exactly where to stick the knife.

But she also drifts closer, like there's some magnetic force between us. The same one I've been fighting since I spotted her on her knees at baggage claim.

Only now I'm supposed to play the role of dickhead brother's best friend, so I can't do one damn thing about it.

Can't reach for her.

Can't explain.

Can't fix this.

"Seriously though," Charlie continues, "are you having a stroke? Because your eye is doing that twitchy thing."

"My eye is not—" I catch my reflection in a nearby window.

Son of a bitch.

It's twitching like an emergency broadcast of my inner chaos to the world.

"Don't worry about the parents." Eve's tone carries that scary confidence that usually means someone's about to get crushed to dust. "I've got just the thing to dial them down a notch."

"Dial them down?" Nick's eyebrows shoot up. "Should we be scared?"

"Probably." She grins, but there's steel underneath. "But plausible deniability and all that."

More shuffling in line. More fucking dripping. More of Holly refusing to meet my eyes, scouring the ground at our feet.

Probably looking for my balls.

Listen, I'll take all the help I can get.

"The last time you 'handled' something," Charlie interjects, "Dad's golf cart ended up in the lake."

Eve shrugs, all false innocence. "Total accident. Could have happened to anyone."

"You took out the brake line," Charlie says with a hard roll of her eyes.

"Accidentally."

They rattle on about bullshit while I'm pinned between the wary stare of my best friend and the silent hurt of the woman who's starting to matter way too much.

Hurt I can't even acknowledge. Because we have a deal, and I'm not adding breaking it to my growing list of failures.

I want to tell her how young and stupid I was, how that mistake is why I know firsthand about staying true to yourself no matter what our parents think—something I sure as shit didn't do.

So many words burn mercilessly in my throat, choking me.

How do I explain being such a coward, so fucking weak, that I married someone I didn't love just to impress my old man?

No, really. How do I—seven years older than Holly, but clearly no wiser—explain how out of the five of us, I'm the one who caved to the pressure? I'm the one who danced.

The only one.

Nick, Eve, Charlie… they blazed their paths. They didn't make a big fuss about it. Just moved through life with easy confidence, knowing they deserved to find their own way on their own terms.

How do I make that make sense for a woman who's spent her whole life on the complete opposite end of the spectrum, spending every moment railing against the very idea of falling in line?

Drip.

The lift creaks overhead as we get closer, the sound grating on my last nerve. Each metallic squeal sends another spike through my temples.

Holly's shoulder brushes mine, and my blood surges. Nothing more than a brush of our jackets, and my cock swells in my pants.

The same way it did as I watched her volley verbally like a goddamn queen this morning with that champagne flute perched daintily between her fingers.

While I sat there and pretended I didn't give a fuck that they ignored her. Literally walled her out of the conversation entirely.

That's the job, right? What better way to look like I hate her than pretending to be one of them.

Drip.

Holly's perfume drifts up, not as subtle as vanilla but not as sweet as birthday cake. Something uniquely her that makes my mouth water and my hands itch to grab her.

To pull her close.

To—

"You know," Eve says carefully, "if you need to talk about—"

"I don't." The words come out sharper than intended, edged with the desperation clawing at my insides.

Charlie whistles low. "Wow. Definitely having a stroke."

Drip.

"I'm fine." Another lie. Sure, my failed marriage was more a lie by omission, but a lie nonetheless.

"Next!" The lift operator's voice yanks me out of the bullshit stew I'm drowning in.

Almost there.

Just need to make it to the Shred Shack with Nick.

Like old times. When things were simple. When I didn't feel like I was being torn apart from the inside out.

"Hey, mister?" a high-pitched voice pipes up. One of the snowball terrorists points above our heads with a grin. "Mistletoe!"

Son. Of. A. Bitch.

Holly gasps next to me and fuck if I know what it means. She wants me to? She'll slice off my balls if I try?

Drip.

"You gotta kiss her!" The kid bounces on his feet, clearly thrilled with his role as mistletoe enforcer.

Not that either matters. We hate each other. That's the deal.

Only I'm doing a bang-up job at turning our ruse into real fucking hate.

"You want to live long enough to see adulthood?" I growl, my voice rough with barely contained violence. "Shut it."

His friend chimes in. "You chicken?"

"Nope, I just don't take orders from a kid who hasn't even gotten his big kid ha—"

"Chance!" Nick snaps, exasperation heavy in his voice.

Drip.

"What?" I spread my arms wide, spoiling for a fight. Desperation and anger mix in my blood like gasoline and lit matches.

"It's not like you want me kissing *her*," I say, jabbing a finger in Holly's direction, but doing every damn thing to not actually look at her. "You're under the damn thing too. You want a piece of this?"

Nick, about done with my shit, leans in with a dose of pissed-off of his own. "If it keeps your lips off my sister, pucker up, buttercup," he says, tossing the challenge out and calling my bluff with all the confidence he'll win.

Well, if my day is fucked, so is his.

"Fine."

Before reason can save me from myself, insanity grabs the wheel with an enthusiastic—*I've got you, bro!*

Grabbing the front of his jacket the same way Holly had me by the dog tags yesterday—I ignore the shock launching his eyebrows to his hairline and plant one on him, quick and hard.

When I pull back, his expression lands somewhere between horror and hysterical laughter as he wipes his mouth with the back of his glove.

"Well," Eve drawls into the stunned silence. "I've gotta say, seems like a waste. Guy-on-guy action should be way hotter than whatever that was."

Charlie makes a gagging sound. "Now I can't kiss my man without kissing my brother. Fucking great."

"Stupidity *and* self-destruction. Good plan," Holly's voice cuts through the chaos. "Throwing tantrums now? Maybe you should be following daddy's commands if you can't be a goddamn adult."

Bulls—fucking—eye.

Just when I thought I'd maxed out on shame. Apparently not.

She's never enlisted, but she sure as hell has the precision aim as though she did—her ammunition? Military grade.

Her words tear through me, through defenses I didn't even know I had left. Because she's right. The first night, I lay there, feeling her tentative touches, listening to her whispered subtle confessions—and I was too much of a coward to even let her know I was awake.

Too afraid of what it meant that her fingertips on my skin felt like coming home.

The same coward who got married so he could prove he was some big swinging dick of a son who deserved his father's respect.

But this?

Holly seeing that weakness? It guts me in a way Noelle's betrayals never could because Noelle was hollow—something that looked solid but crumbled at the first touch.

Holly is steel and fire and unflinching truth. She sees right through every carefully constructed wall to the fear underneath.

And now I know she finds me lacking.

The lift operator waves us forward. Thank fuck. Because I can't breathe under the weight of her contempt. Can't stand replaying every brush of her fingers in the dark while she pities me.

More lies. So many lies.

"Dad's comment mindfucked you hard." Charlie's voice has lost its edge, replaced by something too close to sympathy.

Drip.

"I'm fine." The words come out strangled.

"Yeah, that's why you just rage-kissed my boyfriend." She crosses her arms. "Totally screams 'fine' to me."

Nick is still occasionally wiping his mouth with the back of his hand. "For the record, that was a solid two out of ten. No tongue, no passion. Holly gives better kisses to her coffee cup."

"Can we not discu—"

"Oh, we're absolutely discussing this." Eve's grin is predatory. "I'm thinking diagrams. Maybe a PowerPoint."

The lift operator clears his throat. "You folks riding or writing a romance novel?"

"Ladies," I gesture to the exit ramp, my movements jerky with tension. "This has been fun, but—" I throw my arm out, blocking the girls' path. "No sisters allowed."

"Seriously?" Charlie's voice could strip paint. "What are you, twelve?"

"Generous estimate." I force a smirk I don't feel, my face tight with the effort.

Better they think I'm being childish than see how Holly's words hollowed me out. How the shame burns in my gut, mixing with the memory of her soft touches that I was too afraid to acknowledge.

Eve's eyes narrow. "Back to this bullshit?"

"Just maintaining tradition." I keep my arm firmly in place, even as everything in me screams to let Holly stay.

"Being a dick and running away," Holly fires back. "But hey, at least you're on brand."

The words hit their mark because she's right. I am being a dick. But it's better than the alternative. Better than admitting I can't trust myself around her.

I make the mistake of looking at her. Really looking at her.

The hurt in her eyes makes it virtually impossible to breathe.

My lungs seize.

This isn't just about my father's comment or Noelle or any of it. This is about me pushing her away.

Again.

Just like we did all those years ago.

"I'm not running." The lie is bitter on my tongue. "I'm—"

"A coward."

Drip.

Charlie sucks in a rough breath. "Fuck, Hols."

Without another word, Holly skis out of the line, head high.

"Masterclass in fucking up," Eve mutters.

"Glad you made it to the show." A growl of pure frustration grinds in my throat. I don't need the fucking judgment. I'm doing just goddamn fine with it on my own.

Charlie glances between Holly's retreating form and me. "For someone who's supposed to be good at strategy, you suck at this."

With a shake of my head, I push off and line up for the lift. One look over my shoulder confirms which side my sisters are on as they head off in the same direction as Holly.

Nick flips the metal arm down as soon as we settle on the bench and begin our ascent.

Each grinding foot dragging us higher, even as I've never sunk lower.

Holly's always seen straight through everyone's defenses. A master at reading people and brave enough to call people on their bullshit with deadly accuracy.

And now she's seen through mine.

My hands shake as I grip the safety bar.

"You know what the difference is between you and Holly?" Nick finally breaks the silence as we near the top.

I don't want to know. But I ask anyway, my voice rough. "What?"

"She's the first to apologize for what she does, but

she never apologizes for who she is." He studies my face. "Maybe you should try it sometime."

And that's exactly why she deserves better than me.

12
Holly

Well, slamming my fingers against the keyboard with increasing force isn't working. So much for the hope that pounding the keys hard enough might scare the computer into cooperating.

For the sixth time in twenty minutes, the Wi-Fi drops, taking my presentation updates with it into the digital abyss.

"What did that Mac ever do to you?" Charlie asks from her perch on my bed, swirling her cocktail. She showed up ten minutes ago with fruity drinks—and concern.

I took the drink—shrugged off the concern.

"Nothing yet, but the night is young." I jab viciously at the refresh button. "And this Wi-Fi is personally victimizing me."

The bedside lamp's soft glow casts shadows throughout the room, making it feel smaller, more intimate. Like the kind of space where secrets slip free.

Or where you hide from them.

Charlie takes a deliberately casual sip of her drink. "So… rough day?"

I snort. "That's what we're calling it?"

"I meant the computer, sorry."

"Just technical difficulties." I try for breezy, miss by about eight emotional octaves, and land somewhere between strangled and hysterical.

"And judging from Santa's precision when dropping his sack of computer glitches, he has no problems hitting the bowl."

"Mm-hmm." She studies me over the rim of her glass. "And this… frustration has nothing to do with my brother?"

"Nope." There's that emphasized pop again. "Nothing at all."

"That's good, then it definitely has nothing to do with a certain blond bombshell who crashed?"

"Please." The word is more of a cracked yelp.

A dying seagull.

Helium-like, but solid.

But I totally stuck the landing.

Judges would totally give my graceless swan dive into life's unflushed toilet a solid 8.3.

Ahhhhh, a solid foundation of skills I can build on.

"I couldn't care less about GI Joe's blast from the past."

"Right. And I'm sure finding out about his ex-wife had nothing to do with you bailing on dinner tonight."

"I was working." *Click, click, click, fucking click, thwac-ccckkkk.*

"MMA style from the looks?"

"Don't knock my cardio. Maximum calorie burnage and barely breaking a sweat."

Charlie laughs, but it's not the goddamn guffaw I need.

It's gentle. Understanding.

Which somehow makes everything hurt even more.

"Holly…"

"Don't." My voice cracks. "Just… don't."

The walls close in, squeezing until every insecurity I've tried to bury comes bubbling to the surface. "How did I not know?"

She sets her glass down with a soft clink. "It's not exactly his favorite topic."

"That's not the point." The frustration building in my chest threatens to choke me. "I've known him my whole life. How did I not know he was married? And divorced?"

"Because you were away at school when it happened. And after… well, it wasn't exactly dinner table conversation. None of us even met her."

"Even Sierra looked like she knew." The bitterness in my voice surprises even me. "But I guess they're still friends. Secret handshake, probably."

I spit the words out, skidding to a complete stop before adding bootie calls and dickie dunking to the list.

The very picture of restraint.

"Holly…"

"It's fine." I drain my glass. "Clearly, blondes have more fun. And better Wi-Fi, apparently, because this"— I gesture at my laptop's black screen— "is seriously starting to feel personal."

"That's not—"

"Charlie, really… I'm used to being the one left behind." I slam my laptop closed harder than necessary. "Story of my life, right? Always too young, too loud, too… much."

"That's not—"

"Seven years, Charlie. There are seven years between me and Chance. You and Eve sit in the middle, so you get to slide right in with the guys whenever you want. At best, I get a clear view to watch from the sidelines."

Charlie's quiet for a long moment. "Is that what this is about? Still feeling left out?"

"Yes. No. Maybe." I drag my fingers through my hair, frustrated with my inability to articulate this ache in my chest. "How can I ever expect Dad to take me seriously when I can't even get Chance to stop shoving me back to the kids' table?"

"Holly—"

"And I know it shouldn't matter. I know I shouldn't let it get to me. But…" I swallow hard. "I can't have this in my head during—this week."

I stop just in the nick of time. I can't tell her. Not that I don't trust her—I do.

I love what I do. I'm fucking good at it. I'm not self-conscious, per se. I'm just easily distracted.

My brain drags the smallest observations and details in for rapid-fire processing.

If I tell them, just knowing they're waiting on the sidelines to see the outcome is a distraction I can't afford.

All the things I'm not saying, but desperately want to, try to bubble to the surface.

And Charlie knows I'm holding back. I can see it in her knowing gaze aimed at my lap where I'm wringing my hands.

Needing the immediate safety of distraction, I flip open my laptop and try again.

The Wi-Fi icon mocks me with another disconnection.

Growling, I jab at the keyboard again.

Charlie pulls out her phone. "That's it. I'm calling Nick."

"What? No—"

But she's already dialing. "Hey, handsome, I know you're busy, but Holly's Wi-Fi is edging her hard..." She winces. "Sorry, not the best choice of words. But yeah, she can't stay connected for more than two minutes... a virgin at a strip club has better stamina..." She nods at whatever he's saying as though he's right in front of her. "Uh-huh... Yeah, good idea. Definitely ask him."

My stomach drops. "Who him?"

"The cyber guy, of course."

"Charlie, don't you dare—"

She holds up a finger. "Disconnect? Yeah, she's got that covered." She tips her phone away from her mouth. "Nick says Chance will be right up. Don't touch anything until he gets here."

"I don't need his help."

"Level with me, Hols." Nick's voice carries through the speaker. "If your hesitation is awkwardness from witnessing the kiss he and I shared earlier, just know it was a onetime thing you'll never have to witness again. It's not him, it's me. He assured me it's not me, it's him. Just two ships passing in the night." Nick's full-bodied laugh rumbles through the phone.

Despite myself, my own laugh catches me by surprise. "I hate you."

"No, you don't. Look at it this way—payback for being a prick can start here."

My heart stutters at the sound of the knock on my door.

"That's my cue. I'll see you in a few, babe." Charlie ends the call and bounces off the bed with suspicious enthusiasm. "Try not to kill each other."

She throws open the door to reveal Chance filling the frame, laptop tucked under his arm.

The sight of him sends an unwelcome flutter through my stomach.

"Here for the Wi-Fi issues." His voice is carefully neutral.

"Right, just the Wi-Fi issues. Got it." The words slip out before I can stop them.

"I didn't mean…" He scrubs his hand down his face.

"Never mind." His ordinarily mischievous blue eyes are filled with defeat.

The tired kind I'm intimately familiar with that comes from fighting battles you've already lost.

13
CHANCE

Nick's words rattle in my skull. *Remember what I said.*

A precision-aimed, last-chance warning shot I definitely don't deserve.

There'll be an apology.

I shift my laptop under my arm like it's body armor.

Yours, not hers. In case there's any lingering doubt who fucked up.

He claps me on the back—not a friendly *atta boy* or even a *don't die out there, soldier,* but the kind of clap that feels like getting tagged by a linebacker. To anyone watching, it probably looked like your standard bro tap.

But the weight behind it?

A not-so-gentle *fuck this up, and I'll bury you.*

Nick calls out at the last minute and I glance over

my shoulder, waiting out the man I respect the most in this world.

I don't ever want to see that look in her eyes again, Chance.

His clenched jaw and worried eyes tell me he doesn't like being in this position any more than I do.

If I do, you better pray you're not the one who put it there.

On my way out of the room, the mistletoe catches my eye, dangling right where it's meant to be—but looking suspiciously rough around the edges.

Like it went on a covert mission to the super lift to make sure I got another dose of Holly.

Like I'm not addicted enough after the brief kiss she planted on me.

On a technical level, her kiss and the one I dropped on Nick were virtually exact.

In terms of impact, Holly's hit with the same raw power of a precision-guided missile—rewriting the goddamn rules of physics on impact.

Now, almost outside Holly's door, that conversation feels like a premonition. Every step closer to her room sets off warning bells in my head—the kind that usually precedes an ambush.

When I knock, the sound echoes like artillery fire, sharp and jarring in the quiet hallway.

Charlie opens the door. She smiles, her eyes softening. "Don't fuck this up."

My heart knocks hard.

She knows that we're—there's something—I don't even know. But Charlie definitely knows.

Maybe she could help me figure it out.

"Understood." I can't help but smile down at the little hellraiser. Tough as nails on the outside—

"I love you…"

"I sense a but," I say, adjusting the laptop under my arm.

"You are the butt." She squeezes me in a quick hug. "You're a damned good brother so I'll overlook it."

She glances over her shoulder and turns back to me, schooling her features, but I caught the worry. "Now, before I leave you alone with her, did you seek professional help for your stellar meltdown earlier?"

"You could say that. Nick and I were at the bar when you called."

"That works." With a pat on my chest, she rises onto her toes to kiss my cheek.

"Play nice, kids," she calls back with a wave as she slips out the door.

It clicks shut with an ominous finality. Or maybe that's just the weight of everything unsaid pressing in.

The soft lamplight wraps around Holly where she's curled in the chair, an oversized sweater swallowing her small frame.

Striped socks, baby blue and ivory this time, hug her legs all the way to mid-thigh.

Her glasses catch the light as she glances up, then quickly away.

The room feels smaller than it is, intimate in a way that makes my pulse quicken. Some sitcom plays quietly in the background—*New Girl*, I think—but all I can focus on is how she bites her lip while pretending not to watch me.

"Heard you were having Wi-Fi issues." I aim for casual, miss by a mile.

"That's not all I'm having." The words hit their target with deadly accuracy.

Closing my eyes briefly, I take the hit. When I open them, she's still there, still beautiful, still hurt. "Yeah. We should probably talk about that."

"There's nothing to talk about." She sets her laptop on the table next to her, getting to her feet. "I just need working Wi-Fi."

"Holly—"

"Don't—" She snatches off her glasses and pinches the bridge of her nose. "Can you please just fix the internet and go."

"Yeah. Internet. Fine." Nothing personal, just get her back online and be on my way.

Snagging the seat across from hers, I pull out my gear. The sooner I get this done, the sooner I can go right back to the part I promised I'd play.

Dickhead Duty under the direct harassment of a goddamn possessed mistletoe drunk on power, while making sure I don't blow past the line of Nick's warning.

Make that warnings.

Because at the moment there are two in effect. The classic *Don't Fuck My Sister Decree* aging like a top-tier bourbon, and the newly proclaimed *Fuck Around With My Sister's Feelings and Find Out Framework* he just rolled out.

"Uh, Chance?"

"*What?*" It's more a snarl than a response, but I'm getting warmed up for my shift tomorrow.

She rears back and I immediately regret my tone.

Cocking her head, her eyebrows pitch to the *and just who in the hell do you think you are* position.

"I was going to warn you the vein is throbbing again, but fuck it, let the thing explode for all I care." She's equal parts determined kid I grew up with, fiery spitfire fresh off a baggage claim, and part boardroom battle ax in her prime.

In the face of all of it, there's just one thing to say.

"You try rebooting?"

I've never been a bigger idiot in my life.

"Of course I tried rebooting. Maybe someone should *reboot* you. But in the interest of solving the current problem, I also tried praying, swearing, and threatening the damn thing with frequent flyer miles, destination straight out a goddamn window. Any other stupid questions?"

"Sounds like you've got quite the relationship with technology."

"Yeah, well, at least I'm honest about my failed relationships."

Walked right into that trap.

Hell, I didn't just walk into the trap. I set the damn thing.

Now I can add a brand-new skill to my resume—Proven proficiency at kicking myself in my own ass.

"Right." The elephant in the room demands attention, so I lean back and let the weight of the silence stretch between us. "So you want to talk about that or you want me to fix your connection?"

"Fix *the* connection. *My* connections are just fine." The words come out clipped. Clinical. "The rest…" She looks me up and down. "…doesn't matter."

I bite back my reply because we're here because I fucked up.

There's a price to be paid for it.

For now.

"Alright, then." I nod my head at her laptop. "So sit that sweet little rabid ass of yours back down and let's start."

That sexy mouth falls open before she remembers herself and snaps it shut again. Her hands ball into tight little fists at her sides. "You can't—But I—Dick—"

"I'd ask if a cat's got your tongue, but it sounds less cat and more wood chipper."

"Fuck the internet. I don't need it that bad."

"Bullshit. And you know fuck all about me if you think I can live with tech issues interfering with your winning over Vaultress Global."

At the reminder of what's really at stake, the tension in her shoulders eases, followed by the clenched fists. "I—thanks."

She drags her chair alongside mine and settles in with her leg folded under her.

Otis peaks out from beneath the hem of her sweater.

One glimpse and I'm back to the shitty little room, but the best goddamn place in the world because I'm studying the little guy with her soft thighs wrapped around my head.

She gasps and I follow the direction of her gaze down to the little tattoo. More specifically, my finger tracing over the letters.

I blink down with no recollection of having reached for her to begin with.

Blood surging, the buzzing in my head turns deafening—something inside tumbles and swells.

My chest constricts making my next words a strained rumble. "Just so we're clear, Holly…"

I wait for her to meet my eyes. When she doesn't, I continue to trace over the flamingo with familiar confidence. "The rest does matter."

14
CHANCE

Ten minutes later, we're settled in side by side. "Anything I should know about before I get started?" I gesture to her laptop, desperate to break the tension crackling between us.

She adjusts her glasses, the simple movement sending blood rushing south. "Like what?"

"Well, when I helped Eve, tentacle porn was just the beginning. I'm still traumatized."

Her laugh catches us both by surprise—bright and genuine despite everything.

The second it fades, all I can think about is what I'd trade to hear it again—especially if I'm the reason for it.

Focus, soldier.

With our heads down and tension all but gone, I guide her through the steps to isolate the issue, doing my best to ignore the way she leans in, her shoulder brushing mine.

Her clean, sweet scent is everywhere, sneaking into my lungs like it belongs there.

It doesn't.

But damn, it's hard to remember that.

And then the clues emerge. One by one, each a revelation making my blood run cold.

My mood sours, tension swells, all filling me from the inside out until I'm choking with it.

I shove to my feet and head for the door. Time to have a talk with murder muffin.

She's out of her chair right after me, curling her fingers over my forearm. "Hey, what's wrong?"

"The fucker's hacking your computer."

"Wait, who?"

"Blake."

She jerks back. "What?"

"Look." I head back to my computer and point to the connection attempts, explaining technical details while rage continues to build in my gut.

"You work on my network from now on. Stay here."

Riding the fury fueling me, I'm at her door, hand turning the handle, in four strides.

"Your dad's protege and I are going to have a little chat."

"Oh no, you don't! You're not doing this."

Faster than I expect, she slips between me and the cracked door.

"Chance—no. He's not worth it." Her voice is resolute, almost soft, but razor-edged. Deceivingly delicate fingers curl into my shirt—a tiny act of possession.

We freeze, our gazes falling to where her hand sits now over my thundering heart.

Her chin tilts up, defiant, that same stubborn determination that always set my blood on fire.

Little Holly lived for pushing every last button I had.

Grown-up Holly, she found a whole new set.

"If he gets my files, he wins. If he takes my time, my peace of mind, my confidence… he wins." She sucks in a breath and squares those surprisingly powerful shoulders. "And I'm not letting him win."

"Holly, he hacked your camera."

"Then I guess it's good I watch my porn on a smart TV like a fucking adult, then isn't it?"

The air whooshes from my lungs and an immediate picture forms in my head.

Vibrant blue eyes glazed with building pleasure focused on a large screen. Breathy moans spilling from her lips joining those from the scene she enjoys unapologetically.

Her fingers boldly cruising along her skin, chasing pleasure with absolute confidence she deserves it.

My skin flames hot, but I force my hands to stay at my sides. "I don't like it." My voice is tight, gritty, tortured.

"You don't have to." Her eyes lock on mine. "But you'll respect it."

So much determination in such a small package. "Yeah, I'll respect it."

"Thank you." Her hand slides into mine with the soft-spoken words.

Something just changed. Changed huge. I'm just not sure what.

Settling in beside her, I'm hyperaware of every breath. Fixated on every movement. The gentle slope of her neck as she bends over the keyboard. The way her sweater slips off one shoulder, revealing golden skin that begs to be touched.

Even with the distraction, I have her computer scrubbed and connected to my network—the only way she'll, connect until we leave.

Where I can keep a close eye on that fuckwit sniffing around her father's company.

Days on dickhead duty and nights in close proximity… that doesn't have disaster written all over it.

Not at all.

Not when she shimmies in her chair when something goes right, a little wiggle that makes her breasts sway gently under her sweater. The no-bra discovery pegs the hard-on to one hundred percent, leaving me struggling for air.

An hour passes in a haze of technical jargon and stolen glances. As she fades, her responses come slower, movements less precise, and the yawning starts in heavy rotation.

"I should go." The words feel wrong even as I say them.

"Stay?" She looks up at me through those lashes, uncertainty written all over her face.

"You're wiped out."

"Please?"

Say no. Maintain defensive positions.

No matter what I tell myself, "Okay" slips from my lips.

We end up on her bed, leaning back against the headboard. I stretch out my legs before me. She, on the other hand, curls into a ball, tucking into herself, propping her head against my shoulder.

"Chance?"

"Yeah?"

"It does matter. So are you finally going to tell me?"

She blinks up, the soft glow of the lamp catching on those little gold frames. Fidgeting with the edge of the socks, she runs her finger back and forth rhythmically. Completely unaware how fucking sexy that one little move is by itself, but combined with the socks, devastating.

"I'm so fucking sorry, Holly."

"I know."

"No, you don't, but let me tell you..." I let it pour out. Unfiltered. More than I've ever even told Nick. About Noelle. My father.

About trying so hard to be perfect that I forgot how to be real.

"She looked good on paper," I say, peering down at her, my voice rough. "The perfect military match. Colonel's daughter who understood the life, respected the rank..."

Holly shifts beside me. "So what happened?"

"Paper burns." I release a long, shuddering breath. "Just like anything else."

The silence stretches between us, heavy with the truth of those words. "Six months of pretending to be the man my father wanted, the husband she deserved… turns out paper can't hold up against who you really are."

"And who are you, soldier boy?"

"Someone who's tired of running." I pause, the weight of everything unsaid pressing against my chest. "Someone who's done making the same mistakes."

Her breathing starts to even out, a quiet rhythm that tells me she's drifting off. "I should have told you about Noelle. But talking about her means admitting I was a coward—that I let my father decide who I should be, instead of being who I am."

She doesn't respond, only the soft, steady sound of her breaths breaking the silence. I stay awake, watching over her, each inhale a reminder of everything I stand to lose if I screw this up again.

"Something someone as strong and unstoppable as you would never do."

Her lips move, words lost to the haze of sleep as she curls into me, fitting like she's always belonged there. Maybe she does.

Careful not to wake her, I remove her glasses, setting them on the nightstand. She burrows in deeper with more mumbling, tucking perfectly under my arm.

My phone buzzes.

NICK

Get it figured out?

The double meaning isn't lost on me. I trace my thumb over the velvet-soft skin beneath her eyebrow, marveling at how someone so fierce can be so delicate.

ME

Working on it.

The simple truth is, I feel more for this woman sleeping in my arms than I ever did for the one I promised vows to. The realization terrifies me to my core.

Brushing my fingers along her cheek, I study the sweep of her lashes and the soft curve of her slightly parted lips. "What the hell am I going to do with you, Holly?"

I already know the answer. I've been lost since the closing arguments in the trial of reason versus risking it all—the moment her curious touches, while she thought I slept, cherished me more than anyone ever has. More than anyone's even professed to.

The jury began deliberating our fate with that first kiss under the mistletoe.

She sighs, her arm wrapping around my waist. Burrowing her face against my ribs, she wiggles her nose back and forth before settling into just the right spot.

And the verdict?

Every broken and bruised part of me—my regrets, my desires, every scar and sharp edge—they shift, turning over and locking into place. Not just fitting but finding the answer that's been there all along. The one I was too blind to see until now.

A life sentence, sure. But it's not confinement—it's freedom I didn't know I was capable of feeling.

The scary part isn't how I might fall for her.

It's that I already have.

15
Holly

I wake to moonlight painting shadows across his face and his flannel shirt wrapped around me.

He's still here. Still real. His features soften in sleep, stripped of the careful control he wears like armor. Arm thrown over his head, his shirt rides up to reveal the trail of hair—surprisingly dark in contrast with his dirty-blond hair—disappearing beneath his waistband.

I carefully work my way out from under his arm and push myself up to sitting. He makes a small sound of protest in his sleep, his hand reaching for where I was.

My heart clenches.

This isn't part of the deal—him staying. Him looking like this. Making my heart do that stupid flutter thing that has nothing to do with antagonizing him and everything to do with how his hand found mine in the dark when I admitted my fears about the presentation.

Before I can stop myself, my fingertips hover over his jaw. The stubble has passed the sharp stage, edging into something softer—something that practically whispers, *touch me.*

"You're kind of beautiful, you know that?" I whisper, letting my fingers ghost along his cheekbone. "When you're not being an ass."

His chest rises and falls, undisturbed.

Emboldened by the darkness and the quiet rise and fall of his breath, my fingers trace the arch of his eyebrow—*why does that spot feel so intimate?*—along the slope of his nose, learning him by touch.

My thumb brushes the corner of his mouth, his lips parting on an exhale that sends a sharp shiver racing through me.

"What am I doing?" The words escape, barely a whisper. "This isn't... we're not..."

But we are—something.

Maybe we always have been. Two lives running parallel, separated by time, but always on chaotic courses meant to converge.

My fingers drift lower, following the column of his throat to where his pulse beats strong and steady. His dog tags catch the moonlight, and I toy with the chain, remembering how they felt pressed between us when I kissed him.

"I don't know how to do this." I rest my palm flat against his chest, feeling his heart thud under my hand.

"The whole… feelings thing. Give me a balance sheet, market projections—I can handle those. But this?"

He shifts slightly, and I freeze. But his breathing stays deep and even.

I drag the collar of the shirt to my nose and suck in a deep breath. "You make me want things I shouldn't." The confession slips out, soft and trembling. "Like maybe I don't have to be too much or not enough. Like maybe I can just… be."

My fingers curl against his chest, right over his heart.

"And that's terrifying. Because what if I let myself believe it? What if I let myself trust this—trust you— and it all falls apart?" My voice cracks. "What if I'm still just that kid you guys left behind, only this time it'll hurt so much worse because I know what I'm missing?"

The tear spilling over takes me by surprise, barely making it down my cheek before I'm swiping it away. The darkness and his deep, peaceful sleep no longer feel like a safe enough place to hide.

God, when did I become this person? This soft, vulnerable thing who cries over sleeping soldiers?

"I should hate you for this," I whisper. "For making me feel things. For making me want more than what I've built. For making me…"

Care. Want. Need.

The words stick in my throat, too big and real to voice even in the safety of darkness.

Instead, I lean down and press my lips to his forehead—gentle, barely there. A ghost of a kiss that still somehow feels more intimate than any we've shared.

"This is such a bad idea."

I sink back into the spot next to him. Dabbling with temptation—with what could easily turn into addiction—if it hasn't already.

Curling into a ball, I pull my knees to my chest. It's not much of a barrier between us, but it's something. A shred of distance I can cling to.

But not enough to stop me. Not enough to keep me from reaching out.

Sliding my hand over his stomach, I let it rest there, the tip of my index finger barely brushing his. The contact sends a quiet jolt through me, my skin tingling, my chest aching with words I can't take back.

Even if he didn't hear them.

Even if part of me wishes he had.

"Good night, soldier boy."

The moonlight catches on his dog tags again, glinting like a silent challenge. I close my eyes against the sight. Against the want. Against everything I'm not ready to name.

But the darkness doesn't save me. His presence fills the space between us, steady and unrelenting.

When his hand closes over mine, my eyes fly open. My breath skids to a stop, and my heart pounds so hard, I swear he has to hear it.

Breathing even, his eyes still peacefully closed, he drags my hand up his chest—his movements slow and deliberate, until he traps it under his, holding it steady over his heart.

Thu-thunk… thu-thunk… thu-thunk.

The rhythm reverberates through my palm, each beat grounding and overwhelming at once.

Tomorrow, I'll be myself again. Sharp edges, steel spine, and careful distance.

But here, for now, in the quiet dark, it washes over me—his warmth, his heartbeat, the raw ache blooming in my chest—I let myself feel it all.

16
CHANCE

The bonfire rages too big. The flames burn too bright. The inferno hisses too fucking loud.

At least while I'm forced to watch Everett looking like one of those mountain men in Charlie's romances walking straight off the page and into my business with one goal in mind—hitting on *my woman*.

Yeah, no. Let's try that again.

Not my woman—Nick's sister.

That's better.

Actually, it's fucking not.

That little wearer of fuck-me socks, cute gold-rimmed glasses, and my shirt—*is mine*.

Her secrets—the thigh-high socks she wears at night and the power-packed quotes on white cotton, stretched across one curvy little ass—*also mine*.

And I sure as fuck don't share.

Otis is the exception.

He can keep being my little Harry Potter-inspired sexpot's Hermione, as long as he recognizes I'm ass captain and his little pink ass is riding bitch.

Now, I'm pulling rank on a fucking flamingo tattoo the size of a flash drive—I'm losing my fucking shit here.

It's the boners. Has to be.

Two nights now in her room—a sneak attack case study in how many boners you can get before they kill you.

Every night, Otis mocks me from his front-row seat on her thigh like he called dibs on the best seat in the house to watch the show.

The show?

A goddamn sock.

Where does someone get socks like those *anyway*? And why? Because I'm convinced they're not socks at all. They're the next secret weapon for world domination.

Their superpower?

Striking men stupid and turning us into knuckle-dragging mouth breathers.

This is rock bottom, right? This is how I go out?

Two nights she's asked me to stay, and I do. No protest.

No survival instincts.

Like the mouth breather in flannel over there right now—my shirt is better, FYI—making him goddamn self at home next to her like I won't stop his heart for doing so.

Yup, there he goes, the casual one-leg stretch, nice and relaxed, letting her know she's invited. I've seen these moves hundreds of times. That leg move is only part one.

This is the happy hour straight from hell—how about we get this sleigh ride on the road already, yeah?

Ho-fucking-ho.

Guests laugh in clusters, their voices rising with every passing round of drinks. The only thing able to cut through them all? The maddening sound of Holly's laugh.

Perched on a bench, cross-legged, cute as fuck, and chatting up the bartender, Cleo, with the heavy pour. I plan to keep her busy this week and on Nick's tab. The bastard.

String lights sway from above, casting little orbs of light on Holly's waves. Specifically the ones curling at the ends framing her face. And what the bulbs miss, the firelight catches.

At the moment, it's one of those tempting, soft sweaters peeking out from beneath her jacket.

Near as I can tell, she owns two varieties of those knit tools of sorcery: the kind that slip off her freckle-kissed shoulders... and the kind that invite a hand to get lost underneath.

If Everett even gets a gleam in his eye in the same zip code of getting lost underneath anything other than a fucking avalanche, I'll break his arm clean off and shove it up his ass.

Fucking hell, definitely losing it.

And here comes part two of making moves… in the form of slinging his arm along the back of the bench, where it disappears behind her.

Part three, he'll lean in—yup, there it is. A subtle lean, a funny joke… get her laughing and—what the fuck is that?

Pinching a lock of hair between his index finger and thumb, he methodically rubs back and forth.

That's not *part* of the fucking play. How do I know? I hold the copyright *and* taught it to him.

Plastic digs into my skin at the base of my thumb as the cup crunches in my hands.

Jaw ticking furiously, I gulp down what's left of my drink before I end up destroying the cup entirely, the tight coil lodged in my chest only getting worse.

He offers her his drink, and with a shrug, she settles the cup on her bottom lip and tips it back.

Oh, we're so going to talk about that. I don't care if she thinks she's safe with Everett. Trust no man. Ever.

Her throat works in a series of subtle, rolling movements that shouldn't be mesmerizing—but are.

She does that fluttery thing with her lips and tongue, the little move she does when she's falling at first taste. Then she's tipping the cup back again.

Everett's eyes drop to her throat, his look of interest sliding into a half-lidded gaze I've seen before.

Unfortunately for him, I now have to knock it off his face.

"Plotting a murder?" Nick asks, suddenly at my elbow, all casual judgment and dry amusement.

Fucking funny man.

I snatch the cup from his hands and pour half into mine.

Keep the drinks coming, traitor.

"I'm fine." It comes fifty percent growl, fifty percent snarl, one hundred percent lie—one of many I'm racking up this week.

Nick snorts. "As a finance guy, I have to ask—did you budget for legal counsel?"

"Yeah, that and the money to get you a few kissing lessons." I don't look at him, but the jab lands clean. "Let me know when you're ready to start."

"Talking to the guy is a whole lot cheaper," he fires back without missing a beat.

"Couldn't agree more."

"Put him on notice," Nick says, a smirk tugging at his mouth.

"Smart."

"Get him alone, though. It'll give you the advantage."

"Yes, it will."

"The two-to-one odds are bad enough, but they tend to travel as a pack and—"

"Wait, what? Who?"

"Your father. *Our fathers*." Nick gestures lazily with his

drink, the ice clinking like punctuation. "The four of them are practically joined at the hip."

I blink at him, my brain still untangling itself. "What the hell are you talking about?"

Nick rolls his eyes as if he can't believe I'm this dense. "The missiles you're launching at your dad over there."

His drink tilts again, and I follow the arc of his hand. Sure enough, my father's just beyond Holly, deep in some serious-looking conversation.

Stiff and stoic, he wears an expression that never fails to make my blood boil.

"Missiles?" I ask flatly, though it comes out closer to a growl.

"More like heat-seeking rage drones at this point," Nick corrects. "Hence the financial wellness check."

I let out a long breath, dragging my gaze away from my father and taking a slow pull of whiskey, the burn a poor substitute for the fire building in my chest.

"You've been on edge all night, Chance." Nick's voice drops, less teasing now. "What's going on?" His stare drills into me with analyst precision, like he's running scenarios and calculating probabilities. The intensity of his scrutiny crawls over my skin, leaving me exposed in ways my most dangerous experiences thus far in the Army never managed.

My shoulders bunch under the weight of his suspicion, but I force myself to stay casual, even as his eyes narrow with the kind of focus that says he's picking up details he doesn't like.

My gaze snaps to Holly once again to find her holding open her jacket just enough for him to peek inside.

Gut churning, I count in my head. If I reach three and he's still a hair's breadth from *my breasts*—he's done for.

Just shy of three—his death knell—he throws his head back, laughing at whatever he sees.

Eyes locking on something overhead, his laughter dies, to be replaced by a shit-eating grin. The kind of a man who just stumbled on the goddamn jackpot.

With a playful tug of my hair—*yes, mine*—Holly glances in the direction of Everetts's finger, her brows pinching together.

And there it is. Red bow, white berries.

By tomorrow? Everett's official cause of death.

This fucking thing breeds faster than Nick Cannon.

I see the moment she catches on, her lips parting to argue, but it's too late. Someone in the cluster of people passing by shouts, "You gonna kiss her or what?"

"Or what." Shoving my partially-crunched cup at Nick's chest, blood roaring in my ears, I eat up the distance to them.

Her head whips toward Everett, eyes shot open wide —Jesus, is that good or bad—doesn't matter because, again—*mine.*

The bastard lets out a self-deprecating laugh that ends with a smirk tugging at the corner of his lips.

This is stupid, stupid, stuuuupid.

My boots crunch against the snow as I charge across

the clearing, the buzz of the crowd fading to a low hum. With it, the music takes on new life, the melody distinct, the words clear.

"Oh by gosh, by golly… it's time for mistletoe and holly…"

You have got to be fucking kidding me. Even the songs are in on the goddamn joke.

My brain kicks into survival mode, blaring warning after warning, with the frenzied desperation of scrambling for abort codes as the seconds dwindle down on a bomb.

You're supposed to hate her.

Stay the course.

You promised.

Yup, I did.

I made a lot of promises… but you know what? I did not promise I'd stand by and watch some other guy put his lips where mine belong.

It's not just the usual Everett smirk, either. No, this one is smug. Calculated. He glances at the mistletoe dangling conveniently overhead, then at Holly, and back to me. That bastard.

Holly's head snaps toward me, her expression unreadable—except for the flicker of something in her eyes.

Evidence shows you can become an addict after one hit.

You got that right.

I cage her in without thinking, blocking out the rest of the world. "Don't you have somewhere to be?" I snap at Everett without looking at him.

His smirk deepens. "Nope."

I ignore him. Or try to. Holly tilts her head, her chin lifting like she's daring me to say something. I lean in slowly—too slow—and my nose tucks just beneath her ear. My eyelids drift shut as I take a slow, deliberate inhale. Ah, there it is again—cake, smooth and decadent, drizzled with something rich enough to drown in.

White chocolate, maybe—not too sweet on its own, but topped with something sinfully sweet that's all show, it becomes a slow seduction in liquid form—pure temptation.

A total masterclass in edging—delivered by dessert.

There are helplines for this, soldier. Abort.

But I don't.

Can't.

I drag the tip of my nose along the shell of her ear, rewarded by the jagged hitch of her breath—soft and fragile.

Don't tell her that, though. Holly doesn't do fragile. Not for anyone. Not even me.

The foreign rumble stirring in my throat—low, rough, and far too telling—only exists because she does.

Her pulse flutters against my jaw, a delicate new rhythm, like her body knows something her brain refuses to admit.

And then—just for one brain-melting second—she leans in. Barely. Just enough to make me forget Nick's eyes drilling into me from somewhere nearby.

A puff of breath escapes her lips into the intimate space between us, carrying the faintest hint of something chocolate—sweet and dark, with just enough bite to know it's got a proof rating… all conspiring to drive me over the edge.

"Chance, you don't have—"

I steal whatever she intended to say with the brush of my lips along the corner of her mouth. Slow, deliberate—because I'm a masochist, and I need to know how far I can take this before I lose my mind. It's nothing. A fraction of a second. Imperceptible to the crowd.

But for us—for the two of us—it's everything. Pivotal. Profound. Shattering the paths we've paved, and while we're reeling, pulling us toward something entirely new.

Staggering from whatever just punched me straight through the chest, I honor tradition and kiss her. Keeping it controlled, chaste, enough to pass for nothing more than a harmless gesture and just long enough to satisfy the crowd.

Not nearly enough to satisfy me.

"Tradition's tradition, Squirt," I murmur, my voice steadier than it has any right to be with a storm raging inside of me.

Holly blinks up at me, cheeks flushed, eyes wide— looking like I just knocked her off-center.

Oh, she won't like that part. Not one bit.

Join the fucking club.

The haze possessing us fades away when the crowd bursts into cheers.

Clearing her throat, she narrows those sharp eyes and tilts up her chin—untouchable, defiant—pulling off a record recovery. "Don't look so smug. I give it a five."

Biggest lie she's ever told. And we both know it.

I ignore the tremor in my hand as I snag a whiskey from Cleo.

Act normal.

Just head back to your best bro and pretend you don't want to drag his baby sister somewhere dark and quiet and lose your goddamn mind between her thighs.

The ones haunting me since I woke up with them wrapped around my ears.

I do everything I can to look like Cupid didn't just take a Christmas detour to kick my ass with an evil sprig of mistletoe. Like I didn't just get leveled by the way she looked at me—wide-eyed and breathless—and now all I can think about is getting her under me.

Worse than that?

The goddamn ring flashing through my head.

Platinum—for the boardroom or for running the whole damn show. Pear-cut—soft on one side, sharp on the other. Just like her. A twisted band, one of a kind, a piece of art cradling a diamond nudged into place by fate.

I'm the last man who should be thinking about rings, not after the disaster with Noelle.

But in two fucking days… here we are.

Stealing a hint of the kiss I want before I gave the one everyone else needed… and I fucking destroyed my whole world.

I don't look at him. Can't. Because I have more lies to put on the pile.

For someone who hates liars with every fiber of his

being, I'm doing a bang-up job at becoming a goddamn professional.

Nick's glare cuts through the noise. "What the hell was that?"

"That was my cockblocking service. You're welcome. Everett's cock? Consider it blocked."

His voice drops to a low growl. "And your face buried in my sister's neck?"

I force a casual shrug. Act to keep up and all. "Acquired consent. Because I'm a gentleman."

"Chance—"

I cut him off with a grin that doesn't reach my eyes. "I'm your man on the ground, remember? Doing the dirty work so you don't have to."

17
Holly

Well, shove me in a snow globe, it's a goddamn Pinterest-perfect holiday scene, complete with snow-dusted pines, steaming hot chocolate, nostalgia-soaked parents, and a steady loop of kiss replays so incessant, I need a restraining order.

"All aboard!" the driver calls out, his voice gruff as he adjusts thick leather reins while three massive draft horses stamp their feet impatiently.

Charlie and Nick are already snuggled up like they're posing for a Hallmark card.

My parents naturally gravitated to Chance's parents.

Eve unapologetically took an entire bench and is now studying the wood.

And I am conjuring up my own Christmas miracle in this modern-day, Norman Rockwell holiday hellscape by doing everything possible to forget Chance and his magic, alpha fucking swagger... the motherfucker.

Hic.

That's right, folks, I meal-prepped for this ride to holly-coated hell.

Let's just say when I got in the sleigh, all blood boiling and clit throbbing, I flashed back to the last time in the sleigh and welp—turns out the last time *was* Nicky boy's get-it-on-bang-a-gong ride with the redhead— which is bad enough. But there was the buffet after, and I'm pretty sure he didn't wash his hands so—drunk.

The sleigh's runners creak under the shifting weight as people take their dear sweet time loading for the ride. Cold seeps from the bench through my jeans, biting into my thighs. But I don't move.

I stare straight ahead, the snow-packed path blurring into a smear of white. My only objective for the next hour: sucking down the Devil's cocoa like it's happy hour in hell, and I'm desperately searching for salvation at the bottom of my cup.

Hic.

Every hiccup—a Band-Aid on my existential crisis.

No replaying the way his breath ghosted over my skin. No remembering the tension in his jaw or the way his scent—warm, rich, and infuriating—wrapped around me and settled as though it belonged there all along. Definitely no thinking about the way my pulse betrayed me, fluttering against him like some kind of goddamn secret handshake.

Shut it down, Holly. You've got bigger things to focus on.

Like my drink.

It's a good drink.

"Tradition's tradition," he'd said.

More like a kiss stolen straight from the movies—clit-activating, life-ruining perfection you chase—hungry and desperate for just a little more.

Someone needs to punch him in the pouch and knock him down a peg.

Another sip.

Hic.

Between my clit and Nick's finger bang from Christmases past—two things that should never share a sentence—I'm working up a case-study-worthy brand of PTSD.

But for now, my therapy comes with an octane rating. Way more affordable. The bargain price for this perfect little blur of reality... Let's just check the damage, shall we?

I drag out my own little Love Potion #9 repellent, squinting at the sticker. There's an *S*... I think, actually, give me a minute, it's still moving.

Nope, it's... *a goat*?

That can't be right.

Focus. Numbers. Okay, $20.99! Wait, no—50% off! Jackpot. That's a grand total of... *two goes into nine four times, carry the one but the one is sooooo heavy... Holly's too drunk to math.*

The sleigh shifts, or maybe that's me, and Everett flops down beside me, his face the picture of innocence. "Well, that was unexpected."

Yup. Unexpected.

I catch sight of Chance, the muscle jumping in his cheek as he watches us.

Who the hell does he think he is dropping an Oscar-winning kiss like that on me?

And after two nights of falling asleep curled in his arms while he cracked his stupid, stubborn heart wide open about Noelle and his disaster of a marriage—answering every question I have without hesitation.

Now everything between us is… raw.

Like sushi.

Probably gonna get worms.

His fault. Completely.

But at least he's waaaaayyyyyy over there, stuck sharing a bench with Blake and Sierra.

Right in the middle. Nice and cozy.

Well, isn't Karma just a bitch wearing jingle bells.

I kinda like her.

Karma that is.

Sierra… I'm still on the fence about. Because she's *different.*

Zippety-do-fucking-da.

She got sparklers for nipples or something?

Another gulp and when I lower my travel mug of amazingness, I lock eyes with GI Jackass.

I jut my chin, nodding in bro speak, raising my cup right at him. Judging from his glare, he spots the subtle middle finger. Good. Choke on it.

Am I different enough for you yet, soldier man?

Everett nudges my arm with his elbow, yanking me out of my Chance-and-Sierra death spiral.

"You okay? Because you've got a look."

"Yeah, pretty boy, what look is that?"

"The one that says you're about to drop-kick someone into a snowbank."

My gaze flicks to Chance again before I can stop myself. He's angling slightly away from Blake, which has him leaning into Sierra, and welp, check-fucking-mate.

Bottoms up.

"I'm fine." Too fine. Totally fine. Definitely not replaying a kiss like it's on a goddamn loop or wondering how Sierra *conveniently* ended up right next to Chance.

"Everett, don't you have something better to do?" I follow the question with another deep gulp of Devil's cocoa. Sweeping down my throat, it leaves a sting in its wake on its way to deliver a yummy heat simmering in my belly.

"Not at the moment." His grin sharpens. "Besides, watching this unfold is way more interesting."

"What *this*?" Like I don't know, but still.

He shrugs, all innocence as he leans in, his voice dropping to whisper. "Oh, nothing. Just… whatever it is you and Chance are doing. Or not doing. Your call."

Mid turn, I lose control of the car—*wait*—sleigh.

Nope, I'm not driving the sleigh—the dude in the hat is—or will be.

Maybe.

What vehicle am I in anyway—oooh, my body. I

catch myself with a hand to Everett's chest, my eyes zeroing in on his mouth.

The mouth that would have kissed me looks soft. Playful. Like he'd linger just for funsies. He would never be so rude as to——

A shadow falls over us as Chance looms above, jaw tight, looking like he's ready to go full GI Joe on someone.

His target? From the way he's taken aim with that glare, I'd say he's got his sights on Everett.

Otherwise known as Shred Shack powder pup number threeeeeeeee.

Ha! Sounds like the intro for a bachelor on a game show. Cool.

Hic.

"Well, if it isn't the penetrator extraordinaire himself. Nice pants."

Not that I'm looking at his pants.

Because that would mean I would have to be looking at his Johnny-my-rocket.

Chance's eyebrows shoot up, his glare morphing to shock. Looming over me, hands on his hips, he looks less like GI Jackass and more like—Daddy!

When there's not two of him that is.

Now where was I? Lips. Everett. Yeah. I wasn't done with my assessment.

I force my gaze back to Everett's mouth, but my words are all for Chance. "Problem, rocket man? Powder pup and I are having a stimulating convo, aren't we?" I bat my eyelashes at Everett, I think, unless Chance's twitch is contagious.

Either way, I make my lukewarm interest known.

"And your bulge is crashing the party." I give the offending organ a suggestive once-over. Probably all I'll ever see of it. But Sierra probably saw it on account of being different.

Hic.

"You're hammered."

"And cyber wizard here (Sorry, ladies, wand not included. Accessories sold separately) gets it in one. Kudos!"

Hic.

The bulge and I enter a stare-down fit for a western. No blinking, each waiting to see who'll cave and make the first move.

Finally, bulgy boy puffs out his chest. "Ha! I win! Looks like he *is* happy to stuff your stocking, ho-ho-ho your hoo-ha, jingle your bell, or tweak your 'Twas the Night Before Christmas with his giant, half-licked candy cane rod thing."

Hic.

Everett lets out a whistle, a huge grin splitting his face. Not sure what has him so delighted, but *okaaaaayyyyyyy.*

"Okay, that's it. Hand it over."

I lean into the talking bulge, index finger pressed to my lips. "Shhhh—no talking when the ride's in motion."

"We're not moving yet."

Hic.

"Says you, Mister-Can-You-Look-Over-My-Security-Upgrades-Penetration-Specialist man."

Everett barks out a laugh. "And that's my cue."

He winks down at me, so I rapid-reply a wink right back. I think. Hard to tell. Everything went black for a minute. "Toodle-loo, powder pup number three."

He claps Chance on the back. "Good luck, soldier. She's all yours."

"I'm not his, you know," I say, tossing my head back. I'm mine.

All me—*oh*—mine.

Chance drops into the space beside me, his thigh pressing against mine despite the abundance of room on his other side. He settles the blanket over our laps, the warmth seeping into my skin almost immediately.

"Where is it?"

"You tell me. I didn't know you guys could lose it. Isn't it attached?" I bend down to check under his hood—or do they check under our hoods?

I need my oil changed.

Next thing I know, I slide clean off the bench—almost die—until he swoops his arm around me and plops me right back beside him.

The real world is hard. Let him find it himself.

"The alcohol, Squirt. Where's the alcohol?"

"Not telling." A chill races across my neck, sending a shiver rippling through me.

"Knew you'd be freezing," he mutters. "You never did dress for the weather."

"I dress—*hic*—just fine." My head lolls back with the

words, but I catch it before it can fall off. May not be able to operate a motor vehicle, but this body… I've got this.

Another sip it is.

"Give me that," he says, swiping the mug from my fingers.

"Hey, I'm not done."

"Oh yeah, you are. Did you eat today?" He's patting me down and now I really do regret my adult sippy cup because I'm too lit to enjoy it.

The sleigh lurches forward, finally getting the damn show on the road. The jerk acts as a power button, launching my parents into their regularly scheduled, Christmas-themed primetime programming.

"Remember when Holly used to beg to sit up front with the driver?" Mom sighs.

Yup. 'Cause he was hot—my modern-day Almanzo Wilder. Tall, strong, hardworking, blond, wore khaki work pants with all kinds of stuff tucked away in his pockets—my gaze swings to Penetrator Man.

Uhhhh.

Fuck.

"Eat this." He doesn't look at me when he shoves the granola bar in my hand, and that's fine.

It's fine.

We hate each other.

It's how we roll.

Gnawing my way through bite after bite, like a beaver determined to build a dam in one day, I focus on whatever I see that's moving the least.

He shoves a bottle of water in my hands with a stern look. Like he's giving me my meds and waiting me out to make sure I don't hide them under my tongue until I can throw them away.

Fine. Never taking my eyes off his, I guzzle more than half. He'll regret that in about twenty minutes.

The more alert I become—Mad Libs slipping away by the second—the more I fidget.

And along comes the nervous bouncing.

Being this close to Chance is sensory overload. Pretending we hate each other while his body heat seeps into mine—torture.

If he thinks my just sitting there minding my own business was bad, he should have heard the shit running through my head.

We glide through the woods on a wave of off-key carols. By the time the second rendition of "Winter Wonderland" circles around, the brooding prick next to me, carrier of granola bars, confiscator of my fucking drink, clamps his hand down on my thigh.

My spine snaps straight.

High on my thigh.

Like high, high.

Tap, tap, tap, tap...

Way up there.

Right next to—his finger shifts a fraction—*aaannnnnddd*, he's on it.

"Stop," he growls, low enough that only I can hear.

His fingers flex—slow and deliberate—the warmth of his palm spreading like fire through my jeans.

Rhythmic swipes—gentle but utterly electrifying, sending shocks straight through me.

All while in a casual conversation with another guest sitting on his other side, from Virginia or some shit.

He's the very picture of ignoring his best friend's little sister.

But under the bunched-up, heavy wool blanket, he's like his kiss.

Lazily intentional.

Is that a thing? It feels like a thing.

His fingers graze over me now, carrying the same devastating power as when he toyed with the shell of my ear and brushed a kiss over the corner of my mouth.

Edging the fuck out of me without looking like he's edging me, all in front of a PG crowd.

I bite my lip to keep from groaning, but then Charlie, who has a radar for bad decisions, calls out from the front, "Everything okay back there?"

Her tone says she knows *something*, and I could die right now if my pulse weren't currently having an identity crisis.

His hand lands even higher on my thigh, if that's even possible. A casual move that feels anything but.

Suddenly, I'm back in our little room, tracing the curve of his lips with trembling fingers.

The memory rushes in, unbidden and all-consuming, making me shift in my seat as heat creeps up my neck and floods my cheeks.

"All good here. What about you, Holly? Problem?"

His voice is steady, but there's an edge to it—a knowing, teasing challenge.

Yes, there's a problem.

Because I can't stop thinking about the way your heartbeat felt beneath my palm, steady and unyielding, grounding me in a way I didn't know I needed.

Because I admitted things to you in your sleep I can never take back—even if you didn't hear them.

And because the buzz I had going—the one that dulled all the sharp edges for a little while—is gone.

In its place? Your possessive hand, resting like it belongs, making me want to do it all over again.

"Fine," I choke out, but my voice sounds more strangled than confident.

"Just cold," I add and instantly regret it.

Chance's chuckle—low, dark, and utterly unholy—rolls through me, wrapping around my fraying self-control.

"Should've worn a thicker sweater, Squirt," he murmurs, his voice dipping into a timbre that vibrates straight down my spine. "Keep Otis warm."

With just a handful of words, he transports me to our most intimate moments. Lamplight casting a warm glow, and his fingertip tracing the letters on my thigh.

A fleeting closeness that's not meant to endure, yet it still has its grip on me.

Oh God. I need air.

Yes, I *know* we're outside. Shut up.

My leg bounces, the movements growing sharper,

more frantic—like I'm trying to douse the heat crackling between us.

But all it does is make his hand shift again—just a fraction, but enough that my traitorous body perks right up.

"You better stop," he growls, voice low and thick now, amusement softening the edges. Not quite singsong, but dangerously close.

His hand inches higher, curling with the precision of a predator toying with its prey.

My breath stutters, eyelids sinking shut.

It's not the words themselves, but how he says them—gritty, almost reverent. The heat pooling between my thighs becomes molten, and my chest rises and falls in shallow gasps. His arm steadies me as I sway, the dizziness stealing what little sense I have left.

"Mmmmm… That's my girl."

I'm supposed to be the wrong type of woman.

My eyes flutter open, my vision blurry, but coming into focus, and finding Sierra.

So if I'm the wrong type of woman, why is Chance here with me rather than sitting back there with the right one?

18
CHANCE

The barn door groan, the ancient hinges protesting as I shove it open. Wind whips at my back, but it does jack shit to cool the inferno raging inside me.

She better fucking hide. When I get my hands on her, we're having one hell of a talk. Meaning, I'm going to talk and she's *not* going to keep her mouth fully shut while I set a few things straight.

My jaw aches from clenching it, the muscle there jumping with a life of its own. The memory of her staring at Everett's mouth burns me to my core.

She's not interested in him, not really.

I know this.

But that's the thing about betrayal—it gets its hooks in you, and logic doesn't mean shit.

The mingling scents of hay, motor oil, and wood

pull me back to nights of stolen beers and endless stories, back when our mistakes were innocent—forgettable.

Now I'm becoming a fucking pro at the mindfuck variety, the kind of mistakes with the power to destroy everything and everyone I love.

The sleigh sits silent in its corner, that damn wagon still hitched behind it like some kind of witness to what went down tonight.

To my hand on her.

To her trembling.

To her running.

The low hum fills my ears, that familiar sense kicking in—a skill honed through years of dealing with the little stalker dogging our every step, like some pint-sized CIA operative.

And right now, every instinct is dragging me toward the corner.

Maybe the best place to hide is in the very place you were running from. My hand, her thigh, and then some—the fucking sleigh.

Oh yeah, that would be just like her… feeling all the goddamn things, go to the one place where you're forced to relive it.

The tarp over the back shifts, just enough to confirm what I already know.

My boots crunch on the dirt-caked wood, each step closing the distance, the tension coiling with every step.

Taylor Swift's muffled voice drifts from beneath the

tarp. Followed by that little hum Holly does during the bridge.

Always the fucking bridge with this woman.

Grabbing her ankle, I yank hard, dragging her defiant little ass to the edge of the wagon. Her earbuds fall free, hay clings to her hair, and pure fire blazes in her eyes.

Damn, popped the little menace clean out of her earbuds—with the hold she has on me, this won't be the last time.

"What the hell, Chance?"

In one swoop, I climb on top of her, caging her with my knees at her waist.

Catching her wrists, I pin them to the wagon floor above her head. "Don't ever do that to me again."

"Do what?" Her chest heaves, eyes flashing as she bucks her hips under me. "What's your fucking problem?"

"My problem?" I growl, leaning in closer. "My problem is you sitting on that sleigh eye fucking Everett like— Like—" The words tear out of me, raw and honest—too fucking honest. "Like I wasn't right there."

The words I want to say—the painful ones—I choke them back and cling to safety like a fucking coward.

Confusion flickers across her face. "I wasn't—what are you talking about?"

"I'm talking about you using another guy to get to me." My voice drops, rough with fury and pain I'm still choking back. "I mean it, Holly. I won't go there again —definitely not with you. Got it? Never with you."

I hate where that one moment sent me. Back to a time where I caved to expectation and turned myself into a doormat.

And what did I learn?

Sometimes people are just shit… and it has not one goddamn thing to do with me and everything to do with them.

"Why do you care, Chance?"

My gut offers up straightforward logic—don't tell her.

But my heart? My heart is the captain of debate by day, drunk poet by night.

Because you're everything—maddening, challenging, fearless.

You're the only one who can bring me to my knees.

And when I wasn't paying attention, Squirt, you became my entire world.

Digs by day, falling more in love with her by night.

I can't tell anyone. I can't confess to my best friend that I'm so goddamn out of my mind for his sister, if he ever told me to choose between loving her or keeping my best friend—my brother—I'd choose her *every fucking time.*

I bury my hands in her hair, angling her head just right, and pour every ounce of frustration into kissing her senseless.

It's not gentle. Nothing like our careful mistletoe kisses.

It's raw hunger unleashed, days of pent-up tension exploding in one bruising, soul-wrecking kiss.

She makes a sound in her throat, half whimper, half

moan, sending a surge of blood straight to my cock. But the sigh that follows, ragged and full of relief, like she's been waiting for this—for me, for us—her entire life, that's the sound I'll replay in high def for the rest of my life.

She tastes like chocolate and desire and something uniquely Holly that makes my blood burn.

"Rate that, Squirt," I growl against her throat. "I fucking dare you."

Her hands fist in my shirt as she arches up, meeting my intensity. When she rolls her hips, I nearly lose my mind.

Dragging my mouth down her throat, I savor hit after hit of delicious skin, her pulse racing beneath my tongue with every taste.

Behind her ear, she shivers.

Along her collarbone, she moans.

And along the soft swell of her breast above her sweater, she arches up, silently begging for more.

Spanning her ribs, I graze the underside of her breast in slow torturous strokes. So close to where I want to touch, to taste.

Desperate for warm, bare skin, I slide my hand under her sweater.

Because she's mine.

Every smart-mouthed, sock-wearing, impossible inch of her.

I rock against her, chasing relief I know won't come. Not tonight.

Tonight is for next level torture.

The mission? Collect every soft sigh, helpless moan, hungry growl—and lock them up.

No one else will ever get this part of her.

Never.

Pulling back just enough to see her face, I memorize how she looks in this moment—flushed and fierce and so fucking beautiful it hurts.

There's no going back. The look in her eyes tells me she knows it just as well as I do.

When her fingers tangle in my hair, yanking me back to her mouth, the kiss is different—deeper, hungrier, like she's trying to devour me whole.

And I let her.

Christ, I'd let her do anything as long as she keeps kissing me like this.

My dick throbs painfully, demanding more.

Demanding everything.

I slide my hand higher under her sweater, palm grazing the lace of her bra—

The barn door's groan cuts through our heavy breathing.

Nick's voice follows, casual and unsuspecting. "Chance? You in here?"

Holly goes rigid beneath me, her lips still swollen from my kiss. My heart slams against my ribs as her wide eyes lock with mine.

The guilt I've been fighting crashes over me—not for wanting her, never for that—but for lying to my best friend. My brother.

"They said you came in here like five minutes ago,"

Nick calls, his footsteps echoing on the wooden floor. Each step closer winds the tension tighter.

I press my finger to Holly's lips, silently willing her still. Her breath pants hot against my skin, and fuck if that doesn't make my dick throb despite the danger. "Yeah, I'm here."

"You good? You sound…" A pause. "Occupied."

Sweat breaks out along my spine. One wrong move, one sound from Holly, and everything explodes. "Just… give me five minutes, would you?"

"Sierra's missing too." The amusement in his voice makes my stomach turn. "Second time around that particular block, huh?"

Holly's whole body goes stiff, that earlier fire in her eyes dying.

She tries to pull away, but there's nowhere to go with me still caging her in.

The hurt flashing across her face guts me before she locks it down and the mask I fucking hate slides into place.

"Fuck off, Nick." The words come out harder than I intend, raw with frustration and something darker.

His laughter echoes off the walls as the door creaks shut. "Don't do anything I wouldn't do."

The silence that follows drowns us both.

Holly won't look at me, her hands flat against my chest—no longer pulling me closer but pushing me away. The inches between us might as well be miles.

"Holly—"

"Don't." Her voice cracks on that single word. "Just… don't."

She shoves harder and I let her go, watching helplessly as she scrambles out from under me.

Hay clings to her sweater, her hair a mess from my fingers leaving her looking thoroughly kissed and completely devastated.

"It's not—" I start, but she's already running.

The barn door slams behind her with a finality that echoes in my chest. I drop my head back against the side of the wagon, the wood rough against my scalp.

The taste of her lingers on my tongue, a reminder of everything I want and can't have.

Not fully.

Not yet.

I don't know how long I sit there, minutes, hours… it's hard to tell, but eventually my phone buzzes in my pocket, pulling me out of the haze.

NICK

You and Sierra get reacquainted?

The text burns in my gut because he has no fucking clue how wrong he is.

How the recollection of Sierra—of that summer we spent messing around, a couple of dumb kids trying to find ourselves—completely fades when held against just five minutes with Holly.

I won't be going back and rereading old chapters.

I'm interested in the new one.

Her.

I don't answer. Can't. Because every word out of my mouth lately is a lie.

The ghost of Holly's soft sighs haunts me. The way she arched into my touch. How perfectly she fit against me. The little sounds she made that I'll be hearing in my dreams.

My cock's still hard, my body humming with need, but there's no relief coming tonight.

This is my punishment—wanting her, needing her, and having to pretend I don't.

Having to watch her pull away because she thinks she doesn't matter.

This isn't just addiction anymore. This is something deeper.

Christ. How do I keep acting like I hate her by day when she's branded herself into my blood with tonight's kiss?

How do I go back when I know how she tastes?

How her skin feels under my hands?

How she surrenders?

I grab my phone again, thumbs hovering over the keyboard. But what the hell do I say?

Sorry my past keeps hurting you?

Sorry I'm lying to my best friend?

Sorry I can't stop wanting you even though I should?

In the end, I say nothing. Just push to my feet, adjust my painfully hard dick, and head for the door.

Maybe a cold shower will wash away the memory of

her taste—her touch. The way she looked at me before Nick's words shattered everything.

Yeah. And maybe I'll wake up tomorrow and none of this will matter.

19

Holly

Breakfast is already in full swing by the time I make it down to the dining room. The scent of coffee—a lifeline—hits me as all eyes turn toward me the minute I step inside.

Chance sits at the table like nothing happened. Like last night didn't end with him kissing me as though I was the only thing holding him together.

My lips still tingle where his mouth claimed mine. Not a performance kiss, not with his fingers digging into my hip—possessive and demanding. Like he couldn't help himself.

The thought sends panic clawing up my throat. Because this isn't how it's supposed to go.

He's not supposed to kiss me like he's drowning and I'm air.

And I'm definitely not supposed to want him to do it again.

Subtle touches to absolute destruction—both working in perfect synchronization. His hot gaze searing me to the spot with a look equal parts *moth to a flame* and *run for your life*.

And now he's not even *acknowledging* my presence. Nope. He's perfectly content to act like I don't exist. Which, great. Cool. Awesome. Guess we're right back to old Holly.

He definitely doesn't look like he'll show up to my room again, which tracks… old Holly didn't get those benefits either.

Goodbye to those barely conscious moments right before I drift off—the ones where I feel his fingers weaving through my hair, toying with the strands like it's the most natural thing in the world.

My eyes sting, and something I can't let myself examine settles like an eighteen-wheeler in my throat.

Abort.

Latching on to the promise of fresh coffee like a lifeline—and bacon thick enough to mask the anxiety churning in my stomach—I head straight for the beverage station, each step an exercise in looking casual while my insides wage civil war.

The North says *protect the heart*; the South screams *surrender the lady bits*.

I'm not hiding by the coffee.

Nope.

Yes. Actually, yes, I am.

My hands tremble as I reach for the carafe, my skin prickling with a sharp awareness. The kind that says his gaze isn't just on me—it's touching me.

Possessive. Intimate. Like he's staking a claim without a single touch.

The air whooshes from my lungs. Muscle memory takes over—grab mug, pour coffee, don't think about last night, don't think about the wagon, don't think about—

"Holly."

Chance's voice hits me low in the gut, quiet and careful as he steps up beside me. The coffee sloshes dangerously close to the rim of my mug, betraying the tremor in my hands.

"About last night—"

"Don't." The word comes out sharp, brittle around the edges.

I keep my eyes locked on the dark liquid streaming into my cup. Maybe if I stare hard enough, I can drown the memory of his lips on mine.

I can obliterate the echo of raw pain and desperation in his voice when he thought I used Everett to make him jealous.

I can forget how with every kiss, I declared I would never do that to him again, as though this was only the beginning—not the end after a flash so hot it's left its permanent mark.

"You promised to keep up your end of the deal. Think you can manage that, playboy?"

Oh God—I meant soldier boy. Why did I call him that?

He's silent for a long moment—long enough that I make the mistake of glancing up. His jaw ticks, a telltale sign he's fighting for control.

Good. Let him fight. I spent all night doing the same. Lying in my empty bed, replaying every second of that kiss, wondering how his pain could feel so much like my own.

"Fine." His voice comes out rough, scraping against my nerves. "Whatever you want, *princess*."

Ooooof, that landed.

He knows I hate that word, knows exactly what it means coming from him. But before I can respond, he's already walking away, leaving me with nothing but cooling coffee and the bitter taste of regret.

I slide into my seat, pointedly avoiding Charlie's questioning look from across the table.

Our mothers discuss some karaoke social that—no, absolutely not—they really should not attend. I'll stay in my room, thanks—because who needs that emotional damage.

At least give me a chance to mourn for a year or two, for the death of the single best kiss of my life—until Nick slid in like the damn grim reaper.

I don't even have a cock and he's blocking it.

At the table, Blake's already holding court, carrying on about Asian markets and tech sectors. His voice carries that practiced confidence that makes my skin crawl.

I've forgotten more than he's ever known about tech markets. But this is the shiny new toy, and he's excited—overconfident, pompous, cocky—pick a word.

All apply.

Finally, I have to cut in, because the information he's spouting off isn't even from this quarter—it's from last—and life is too short to suffer this tool.

"If you look at the *fourth* quarter projections, there's a clear downward trend in—"

"Holly, dear." My father's voice slides in smoothly, carrying that note—the one that sounds warm and paternal to outsiders but lands like a pat on the head to those who know better. "Blake has a real knack for navigating the complexities of tech markets. He's one of our greatest assets. You might pick up a thing or two if you take a step back and listen."

Normally, I'd let it roll off my back. A lifetime of pats on the head and dismissive smiles trains you to absorb condescension like a sponge all while praying it doesn't seep into your bones.

At the beginning of the week, it was even kind of funny. Ridiculous, but distant enough not to sting.

But now? Now it's not funny. Now it's infuriating.

I can't keep sitting here, expecting everyone else to change. I can't keep waiting for my father to wake up and see me as more than the polite applause at the end of his big show.

So, what if I'm supposed to start changing first?

Maybe the first step is making daddio take a step back.

"Yeah, he's a real rock star," I say, my voice syrupy sweet.

Must be why he *didn't* pick up my emphasis on fourth.

You can lead a horse to water, but you can't make him drink, huh?

I beg to differ. This fucker, Blake, can't even be led to the damn water.

I prop my chin in my hand, the absolute picture of mocking interest. "Please, don't let me stop you. There is nothing quite as fascinating as *third*-quarter projections in the *fourth* quarter. I look forward to hearing the histories from such a savant of the markets."

The familiar ache is still there in my chest—but smaller.

My father's a bit smaller too.

I glance at my mother, noting the subtle tension in her shoulders. It's almost imperceptible, yet it feels like a warning. Truth is, I don't really know her—not the way a daughter should.

I know the woman she shows the world: the capable social wife who caters to my father's every need, so polished and poised you'd think she was born that way. But now, watching her study her plate as if it can solve the quiet battles she's been fighting alone for far too long. I'm realizing there's a whole other side to her.

Maybe there's a part of her that's sick of this shit too.

Something shifted last year when Nick confronted

her about the way she treated Charlie. It was small at first—like the edges of her carefully tailored persona had started to fray. Now, as she tries—really tries—to mend those broken parts, new cracks are forming, letting me glimpse something raw and real beneath the surface.

I don't know yet what that something is. But I can feel it. It's changing her.

And it's changing me, too, because it makes me want to know her in a way I never have before.

Maybe she feels the same, but she's lost about where to begin.

And maybe that shared uncertainty is our common ground.

When I finally let my gaze pass over Chance, definitely not stopping to linger—armor's in the shop and all—his expression remains carefully neutral.

But there's something in his eyes I can't read—but weighs more than my father's condescension and Blake's barely concealed derision combined.

Everett strolls in then, hands casually tucked in his pockets. "What did I miss?"

Don't ask—you're the lucky one.

The men shift back into their conversations, and just like that, the sharp edges in the air dull a little. My father picks up where he left off with Blake, and even Nick and Everett fall into their usual rhythm, with Chance eventually joining in.

I push back my chair, keeping my movements casual, and reach for my cup. I've got a few asses to kick, they won't kick themselves—although the picture in my head of them trying makes me laugh.

Instant relief.

I'm halfway to the sideboard when Chance's voice cuts through the low hum of conversation.

"Hey, sugar lips," he says, his tone loud enough to catch everyone's attention. The hum of conversation dies instantly. A low murmur of surprise ripples through the room, and all eyes swing toward me.

I turn to him and somehow manage to keep my voice low and steady, but heat is already rising in my chest. "What did you just say?"

Unease rumbles through the air. Nick strangles his fork in his fist—brotherly instincts overruling friendship—his most scathing warning glare locked on Chance.

Charlie and Eve flank Nick with looks of fury mixed with a good dose of disgust.

I'm not alone in this. And it's something.

"You heard me," he says, nodding toward his bowl. "You mind taking care of this for me while you're up?"

Blake smirks with amusement from across the table, clearly enjoying his front-row seat to this little misogyny fest. It's exactly his speed, and he looks ready to order popcorn.

My stomach twists, the humiliation churning violently in my stomach, the coffee turning rancid.

It's not just what he said—it's the way he said it. Like I'm nothing. Like I'm supposed to smile and nod. Don't make a scene. Just grab the dish.

But it's Chance's expression that cuts the deepest—

so damn casual, like I'm nothing but a convenient afterthought.

I see my mother in my head, delivering my father's meals. And when he walked away, leaving his dishes behind, she'd swoop in and think nothing of cleaning up after him. After all, he was the breadwinner building a legacy.

And if that's what she wanted, what she was happy with, I have no problem with that.

But what I keep circling back to over and over is how he never thanked her. Not once do I recall him acknowledging her show of support—not one single time.

"You're right. I *am* already up."

"Appreciate it, peasant." He drums his fingers. The picture of casual. Nowhere to be—but in no hurry to get up and do such a menial task.

I pop my head just outside the doorway where I remember seeing John working, hoping he's still there.

"Good morning, John." I flash him a genuine smile. He has no idea how his very presence just made my damn day. "You mind?" I gesture to the hammer hanging from his belt. "I'll bring it right back."

"Is there something I can do—"

"Nope, will only take a minute and you're a busy man."

The minute I grip the offered hammer, the weight just feels right in my hand—solid, real, grounding.

The rage builds in my chest, hot, sharp, and unstoppable.

Because this isn't just Chance being an ass. This isn't

just him trying to keep up appearances. This is every moment I've fought against, every expectation I've tried to break free from.

And coming from him—after last night, after everything—it's worse somehow. Like he reached inside me and found exactly where to twist the knife.

"Holly." Nick's voice carries a warning, but I barely hear it.

With all the encouragement of the *don't get mad, get even* panties I chose this morning, I bring the hammer back, and in one confident swing, I execute the perfect arc—landing a precision hit.

Because I get shit done.

GI Fuckwit should be able to appreciate the beauty of nailing it.

Shards scatter across the polished table among a chorus of gasps—shattered expectations glinting in the morning light.

A deep scar splits the wood where the hammer struck—a lesson and cautionary tale.

Hands flat on the table, the hammer pinned under my palm—the way I was pinned under this son of a bitch last night, I lean in real close.

Just so we're fucking clear.

"And that's the last time you'll ask me to take care of your bowl." My voice comes out steady, calm, even as my pulse pounds in my ears.

Pushing off the table, I head straight for John. "Thank you, sir. I appreciate it."

He rewards me with a knowing grin and a shake of his head.

Behind me, I hear Nick's voice, low and sharp, "What the hell is wrong with you?"

But I don't stop and listen for Chance's answer.

I don't turn back. Because some lessons are worth the price of fine china, and some scars need to be visible —carved into mahogany and memory—to remind us why we can never go back.

Let them see that scar for years to come. Let them remember the day Holly McAdams decided she was done being what everyone else wanted her to be.

20
CHANCE

Holly's righteous fury radiates off her in waves, and fuck if it isn't the hottest thing I've ever seen,

And most heartbreaking. Because I delivered the kill shot.

My cock strains against my zipper, proving once again that my body has zero respect for appropriate timing or brotherly loyalty.

I went too fucking far. I knew it from the minute "sugar lips" came out of me.

She saunters out, hips swaying, head held high, taking the stunned silence with her.

Everyone begins talking at once. Between our moms, Charlie, and Eve, it's a storm of commentary…

You should check on her.

No, you should go check on her.

Mom, she's fine.

That's the most fine I've ever seen her actually.

It's Chance you should worry about; he's going to need a bodyguard.

Eve whips around in her chair then, her face screaming *look at this fucking idiot.* "I'm sure you haven't planned for this, but on account of you being a moron… what's your preference, cremation or burial?"

My father tries and fails to hide a grin behind his coffee cup.

Wait, grinning?

Okay, stick a pin in that for later because on my other side Nick hasn't said a single word and instead pierces me with a dangerous intensity, anger rolling off him.

And me?

I'm drowning in guilt for playing into the exact thing she's fighting against, even if it was meant to keep our cover.

I panicked. Seasoned soldier, known for his level head, and I choked under pressure.

Risking a glance, I see an expression I never expected from my best friend. Nick staring at me like I just crossed a line I'll never be able to cross back over.

"I need air." I shove back from the table, the chair scraping against hardwood like a scream.

"Yeah, you do." Nick's voice is low but firm, his chair creaking as he stands. My gut clenches as I hear his footsteps close behind mine.

"Nick—"

"Keep walking," he snaps, his voice tight and brimming with fury. When we round a corner, he jabs a finger toward a side door along the hall leading to the locker rooms. "In there. Now."

The minute the door snaps shut behind us, he rounds on me. "What the fuck was that?"

It's a tone I've never heard from him before. A cutting snarl I hope I never hear again.

I drag my hand down my face, looking away—lies are easier when you don't have to meet someone's eyes. "It's not what you think."

Except it is.

I made her a promise, and walking this tightrope—constantly worrying they'll see right through me—is exhausting.

The Army trained me for a lot—strategy, survival, maneuvers—but not for this.

And they give us armor.

There's no armor for loving her.

It's fucking big, and I carry it on the outside. Exposed for anyone to see.

All it would take is one slip, one glimpse from the right angle, one second where I'm not guarded, and they'd know.

They'd all know.

I pushed too far. Gave too much away.

After finally tasting her for real, none of the mistletoe shit—it's like I'm walking around with a self-inflicted brand. *Her.*

"Oh, it's *exactly* what I think," he snaps, crossing his

arms. His glare is unrelenting. "This is about Everett, isn't it?"

The accusation knocks me off-balance. I whip my head around to face him. "What?"

"Don't play dumb," he says, his tone edging toward dangerous. "You've been on edge since last night. Since she was cozying up to him on the sleigh. And now this?" He gestures back toward the dining room, his mouth twisting into a grimace. "Jesus, Chance. Man on the ground or not, this is extreme."

I let out a harsh laugh, sharp and humorless. "It's not that and you're blowing it out of proportion."

"Am I?" he snaps, stepping closer. "Because it sure as hell looks like you're trying to warn him off, but humiliating her to do it? It doesn't get lower than that, Chance."

The knot in my stomach twists even tighter. I should correct him.

Tell him he's wrong. I'd never intentionally humiliate her. I'm not that guy. I've never been that guy. If I just tell him how I feel…

But if her father finally chooses her, she wants—no *needs*—for him to choose her on her own merit.

She's stepping into her own… a version of herself who doesn't measure her worth by anyone else's yardstick. After a lifetime of being smacked down, she needs to prove to herself she has the control to determine her course.

She probably doesn't even see it, but she's infusing

her own confidence, making up for where her parents failed her.

She's doing something I wasn't able to do.

I'm not jealous… because I want to see her fully realized too. I'm in complete awe of her recognizing the need to do it and despite any fears she has, any threat of rejection, she's doing it anyway.

The badass in that room who turned on Blake is exactly the strong, capable person she was always meant to be.

Nick stares at me, his frustration giving way to something colder. "You think I didn't notice the way you were glaring at him last night? Or how you've been watching her like a hawk ever since?"

I shake my head, forcing my voice to stay steady. "Nick, you don't know what you're talking about."

"Then *make* me understand," he fires back, his voice rising. "Because from where I'm standing, it looks like you can't handle the idea of her being interested in him. Question is… why? And instead of dealing with it, you're taking it out on her."

Part truth. I can't handle her being interested in him, but we are so far past that.

My fists clench at my sides, and my pulse pounds through my skull with the effort to keep the truth buried.

I want to tell him—need to tell him. If it were anyone but her…

I love her.

I love her so fucking much, I don't know what to do with it all.

She's all frenetic energy, eclectic in everything she does, and fucking amazing.

How the fuck does she not burst into a million pieces?

Because the ache in my bones, a pulsating rhythm that matches the chaos, is relentless and tearing through me every minute.

If Nick experienced even a fraction of this falling for Charlie… I owe him a huge apology for anything I said that made it harder.

"You promised me you'd look out for her," Nick says, his voice quieter now but no less sharp. "But if this is what that looks like? I don't know if I can trust you."

His disappointment is suffocating, heavier than anything he's ever thrown at me.

He shakes his head, stepping back. "Figure your shit out, Chance. And fast. Because some things…" He pauses and shakes his head. "Some things break in ways that change everything."

He heads for the door, then stops. "And Chance?"

"Yeah?"

"If you have any hope of fixing this, the apology better be fucking spectacular."

21
Holly

My chest tightens so hard my breath squeezes out in a whoosh, leaving me lightheaded. I stare at the words for a second longer than I should, heat flaring under my skin.

Damn right, he does. My heart kicks up, betrayal and anger warring with something terrifying I don't want to name. I snatch up the phone again, my fingers trembling as I type.

ME

Gold star for the obvious, soldier boy

CHANCE

Let me fix it.

Fix it? A sharp, bitter laugh escapes me, and way too loud in the quiet room. My stomach twists as I picture the pieces of his shattered bowl. The shards glint in my mind—a warning and reminder of how easy it would be to fall into the same trap as my mother with my father.

Chance isn't my father. I know that. But the pull—the need to prove something—it feels the same. Dangerous. Familiar in all the worst ways. And the worst part? A tiny, treacherous piece of me still wants to try.

ME

Pretty sure that bowl is beyond repair

CHANCE

Not the bowl. Us.

The words slam into me. I collapse onto the bed, my phone clutched too tightly in my hand. My breathing slows, but my heart pounds like it's trying to fight its way out of my rib cage.

Us.

My fingers hover over the keyboard, his words making it sound so simple—like naming it could make it real.

But what if it's already ruined?

ME

> There is no us. There's you being an ass
> and me finally doing something about it.

CHANCE

There's always been an us, Squirt.

It took what he did to finally understand everything he was trying to tell me when he pinned me under him in that wagon.

The pain he must have felt to reach that point. But more than the words he said were the ones he didn't—and how I'm choking back the same ones.

Because a part of me is terrified to do the same. Big terrified. The kind of terrified I'd rather cut out my own tongue than admit.

ME

> Call me Squirt again, and I'll find
> something bigger than a bowl to smash.

CHANCE

Can we talk?

ME

> Talk all you want, soldier boy. I've never
> been anti-imaginary friend.

CHANCE

I want to talk to my real one.

The phone slips in my hand, but I manage to catch it before it falls.

His real one.

My heart surges into my throat, the ache in my chest only gets worse, and I press the heel of my hand to my sternum, trying to ease the throb.

Don't be the next thing I have to get over, Chance.

ME

Room 208. Knock first, he's probably balls-deep in your sister.

It's a cheap shot. I know it, and so does he. The flicker of guilt is immediate, but I push it down, stuffing it deep.

CHANCE

I'll let that slide.

I roll my eyes.

Damn him for always knowing when to ease up, when to give me room to breathe.

And thank you.

ME

How magnanimous you. BTW Otis has a message for ya

CHANCE

Fixing this first. I'll buy Otis a drink if I survive. Ten minutes. Back entrance.

ME

And if I don't show?

CHANCE

You'll show.

ME

Awfully confident for someone who just
got wrecked by dishware 🎯

CHANCE

Some things are worth the hit.

His words dig deeper than I want to admit. My throat tightens as I set the phone down, my hands trembling slightly.

Maybe they are.

I stare at his text until the words blur, debating for the hundredth time whether I should go down there. My fingers linger over the phone's screen, reading through—scrolling up—starting again.

The bowl incident still stings, a raw wound under my carefully crafted armor. But those texts... they cracked something open.

There's always been an us, Squirt.

That hits different.

Fuck it.

The back entrance is quiet, with nothing but the distant thump of bass from the bar and the soft whisper of snow in the air.

I find him straddling a snowmobile, his hands resting lightly on the handlebars, the thrum of the idling engine filling the cold, quiet night. The machine vibrates beneath him, sleek and powerful, and all I can think is that's not playing fair.

The moonlight catches on the shadow of stubble

along his sharp jawline. My fingers itch to trace the line the way I did as he slept.

Damn him.

Definitely *not* playing fair.

The snow crunches under my boots with my slow, deliberate approach, because I'll be damned if I show him the effect this is having on me.

He tilts his head, his gaze locking on mine with an intensity that feels like a full-body check.

"You came," he says, his voice rough, carrying a weight that lands heavily between us.

"Questionable decision-making is a theme for me lately." My voice is sharper than I intend, but I don't soften it.

I can't.

Not after breakfast. Not after he crushed the trust I put in him after he held my hand in the dark and gave me what no one else has given me—what I never knew I desperately needed.

His jaw flexes, his eyes dropping to the snow for a moment. When he meets my gaze again, there's no smirk, no cocky edge. Just the kind of pain you don't admit to. "I'm sorry."

The words hang in the air, visible like the puffs of breath we both exhale in the cold. I don't say anything, just lift an eyebrow, waiting for him to continue.

He shifts, sliding off the snowmobile with a grace that feels too practiced. Standing, he's suddenly bigger and broader, the bulk of his winter jacket making him look even more solid. He holds his ground, though, keeping the snowmobile between us like he knows he's not welcome to come closer.

"You've got five minutes," I say, crossing my arms tighter. "Clock's ticking."

He nods, his throat bobbing as he swallows hard. "I deserve that." His voice is steady, but it's threaded with something jagged and raw.

"And more. I fucked up, Holly. I handled everything wrong. You walked into that dining room, and I panicked. I-I didn't know how to keep it together."

I look away, staring at the snowmobile—it's safer. "You handled it exactly the way I should have expected. You were right on brand, soldier boy."

"That's not fair."

I snap my gaze back to him, heat rising in my chest. "Fair? You want to talk about fair? You humiliated me." My voice cracks, and I bite my lip so hard it stings. "My father had a front-row seat to—I trusted you." My voice catches on tears, but I force myself to face him. "You went way too far today."

"I was still reeling from the night before—then trying to sell the whole hate thing—"

"By destroying me?" The words crack between us like lightning. "I have lines, too, Chance. That's not just one of them. That's a fucking wall."

He takes a step toward me. I take one back.

"You didn't deserve that. You didn't deserve any of it." His words come out low, almost broken. "And I hate that I'm the one who did it."

"Good." But my back hits the actual wall, and

suddenly he's right there, all heat and intensity and regret.

"It'll never happen again, Holly." He fists his hands at his sides, like he's physically restraining himself from touching me. "Ever."

"Then why did you?" The question escapes before I can stop it, quieter than I intend.

It's too vulnerable, too open.

I hate myself for asking, but I need to know.

"Because you scare the hell out of me," he says, the words spilling out fast and raw. His breath fogs in the air, but his gaze stays locked on mine, unflinching. "You always have. But it's different now—Jesus."

He drags a hand through his hair, a frustrated sound rumbling low in his throat. "Those are the same words Nick used when he admitted he was falling for Charlie. He was honest and I'm—I— Lying about this is killing me."

"It's almost over. You just have to—"

"I know," he interrupts. "But then I have to tell him the truth."

My breath catches. "The truth?"

"That I'm in love with you."

The words land like a punch to the chest, sharp and unexpected. My lungs refuse to work, the cold air sticking in my throat as I try to process. He said it. He actually said it.

Every part of me screams to push him away, to throw up every wall I have left. Because if I don't, if I let him in and he screws up again—I'll shatter.

"Chance—" My voice is barely a whisper, and I hate how unsteady it sounds.

"I'm tired of pretending," he says, stepping closer, the snow crunching under his boots. "With him. With you."

He reaches into his pocket and pulls out a key, holding it out between us. "But I'm starting with you, Holly. Starting and ending with you."

I stare at the key, my throat thick and tight. "What's it for?"

"The Shred Shack." His voice softens, and something flickers in his expression—hope, maybe? Or desperation.

"I know what it meant to you, always being shut out of it. I'm done with that, Holly. I'm done keeping you out."

The words crack through something I thought I'd made indestructible. My fingers twitch at my sides, wanting to reach for the key, but not trusting it. Not trusting him.

"Why now?" My voice wavers, but I hold his gaze. Because I need to know. Need him to give me something real.

"Because, thanks to you, I know what it feels like to have the most important person in your world let you in." His voice is low, steady, and painfully sincere. "I want you to know what that feels like too."

I blink, the ache in my chest splintering, but I keep my tone light. "I'm the most important person in your world, huh?"

"Yeah." His lips twitch, something almost like a smile, but it doesn't reach his eyes. "Yeah, you are."

A breath catches in my throat. My pulse stutters and trips because—what the hell do you even say to that?

He takes a shaky step closer, the snow crunching under his boots. "And I can't lose you—not like this. Not because of my own fucking fear."

The ache shifts, softer now, quieter. Waiting. My fingers move almost on their own, brushing his as I take the key. The cold metal presses into my palm, grounding me in the moment as I finally look up at him.

And for the first time since this whole thing started, I don't feel like I'm the one standing on the outside.

"You've got one shot," I say, my voice stronger now. "Don't screw it up."

His lips curve into a small, almost shy smile, and something in my chest stirs. "I won't," he says simply.

I climb onto the snowmobile, gripping the handlebars as he swings on behind me. His arms settle on either side, and the heat of him seeps into me, making my pulse stutter.

"Trust me," he murmurs, his breath warm against my ear. "I've got you."

I almost believe him. Because I'm pretty sure I love him too and I don't want to let him go. I will if I have to—but God, I don't want to. Maybe this time, he'll prove me right for believing.

22
Holly

"Last chance to change your mind, soldier boy."

The words come out steadier than they have any right to. Getting here took three pep talks, two shots of liquid courage, and a stern reminder that I am a grown-ass woman who does not run from her problems.

A six-foot-something problem wielding a key like he's about to unlock more than just the door.

He works the lock with practiced ease. "No more 'no girls allowed.'"

"Not that it was strictly enforced." The words slip out before my brain can pull the emergency brake.

"That's just Sierra. She's different."

"Chance?"

"Yeah."

"Make that the last time you say that."

His swift grin tells me he sees right through me. "Jealous?"

"Bite me."

His gaze slides down to my thighs. "Eventually."

The inside is surprisingly warm, all weathered wood and bare, but strong bones. Along the wall, a twin bed on a metal bed frame dotted with rust, and on the other side, an ancient woodstove in the corner.

A tall window overlooks the valley. "Wow, so you guys really do still come here even now."

"Everett keeps it up." Chance moves to the kitchen area. "Sometimes the weather turns and they crash here overnight instead of pushing it."

He drags a thermos from inside his jacket. Followed by a bottle of liquor.

"Is that schnapps?"

His grin is pure mischief. "Can't have a proper Shred Shack experience without it."

Great. Because what this situation *needs* is alcohol. You know what they say, nothing helps clear up romantic confusion like peppermint-flavored terrible decisions.

And like I said, I've had two shots of liquid courage already.

While he works his magic, I wander the space, studying photos of the lodge throughout the decades. There's something intimate about seeing the place's history, knowing we grew up in these snapshots.

He holds out the thermos lid, filled to the brim with spiked, rich hot chocolate. Definitely not from a packet.

I snatch it free and take an immediate gulp. Anything to hide the tremor in my hands.

Because we're actually here.

Alone.

With his promise to bite me eventually hanging between us. And I don't do good with vague.

Give me a timeline, my man. I'll even take it in military time, with coordinates and a detailed action plan. Maybe some of those tactical maps with the little arrows showing troop movements.

"Go slow, Squirt. No more pimping out my junk to —what was it you said? 'Tweak your 'Twas the Night Before Christmas.'"

The cocoa slides down my airway with a sharp intake of breath.

I pound a fist to my sternum, you know, trying not to die.

Of all the moments for him to bring that up while I'm drinking his horny I-wanna-sex-you-up-in-the-ole-shack brew.

This is how I go out.

Not in some epic skiing accident, but choking on spiked hot chocolate because the guy I've been crushing on decided to quote my horny Christmas poetry back to me.

"I—God, I did say it out loud, didn't I?" I croak out the question, gripping the metal bed frame for support and trying not to drown in my own stupidity.

Eyes crinkling at the corners, he grins and lifts my cup for a sip, turning it so his mouth settles over the lip balm print I left behind. "Oh yeah, you said it." He tilts his head slightly, a wink slipping out like it's second nature. "And then some."

Don't clench your thighs, don't clench your thighs... His gaze drops to my legs where I'm, indeed, clenching my thighs.

Because apparently my body has zero chill and all the subtlety of a neon sign flashing AVAILABLE FOR CLIMBING LIKE A TREE.

"Problem, Squirt."

"You have to stop calling me that."

"Or... and I'm leaning this way, we could just change the reason *why* I call you that."

"If you think I'm taking a ride on your peppermint log here where you diddled Sierra, you are out of your damn mind."

It's his turn to choke now, while I take a seat on the ancient bed, the springs protesting my weight.

He swipes at the chocolate rolling down his chin. "What the hell—I wasn't the one who diddled Sierra here. Might have been a hand job—"

"Oh. My. God. Don't tell me that." Gripping the mattress tighter, I squeeze my eyes shut, doing anything I can to block out the visual.

Come on, come on, give me a retired, social-security-collecting stripper, faded cupid tattoo on her ass, grinding a dildo, mounted on the back of a carousel horse... and go!

"You're the one who brought it up. Just clarifying."

I crack open an eye. "So Nick…"

"Nope. Nick was the first kiss. Everett, on the other hand."

"No way!"

I *am* going to have to overwrite that hand job though —squeeze that tone he uses to say "she's different" clean out of him, right through his jingle berries.

"Yup. And I've never seen two people fuck as much as they do to this day, without actually fucking."

"I hope they changed the sheets since then." Actually, I hope they burned them. And the mattress. Maybe we should be wearing hazmat suits right now.

Running my palms over the mattress, my fingers catch on something tucked underneath. "What's th—"

Chance's eyes go wide. "Don't—"

Too late.

I hold up the vintage Playboy like a trophy. "The sacred texts!"

"Those aren't—" He lunges for the magazine but I dance away.

"What's wrong, soldier? Afraid I'll find your teenage spank bank?" Scoching back, I lean against the wall and flip through pages. "Wow, the nineties were not kind to —holy shit."

"What?" He freezes.

Peeking over the top of the magazine, I raise an eyebrow. "Notes in the margins?" I squint at the familiar cramped handwriting, pretending I can make out the faded letters in the dim light. "Dear Diary, today I learned about the quality of Sierra's hand lo—"

"That's enough of that."

"Oh my God, wait—there's a color-coding system? Did you actually highlight the important parts?" I flip another page, cackling. "Please tell me you made a study guide. 'Chapter One: The Female Anatomy—A Comprehensive Review.'"

He lunges for the magazine, but I'm faster, rolling away, shielding the evidence of his wayward youth under me.

"Was this prep for your oral exam?" I wheeze out between laughs. "Did you get extra credit?"

His face flames. "I was thorough."

"Clearly." I can't stop grinning. "Did you make flashcards too? Pop quizzes? Weekly progress reports?"

He lunges again, but I manage to block him for a second time. My victory lasts approximately two seconds before his weight settles over me, one hand braced beside my head while the other snakes under me for the magazine.

"Getting handsy there, soldier." My breath hitches as his chest presses against my back. "What happened to consent?"

"That was before you found my thesis on advanced female anatomy." His voice rumbles against my ear, sending shivers down my spine. "Now it's a matter of national security."

"What, afraid I'll discover your original hypothesis

on the—" The magazine disappears from my grip as he uses his superior reach to snatch it away, but I'm already rolling beneath him, ready with my next quip.

Only he doesn't move back. He stays there, hovering over me, close enough that I can see the flecks of gold in his eyes. The laughter dies in my throat.

"Hi."

His voice dips intimately low.

"Hi, yourself."

And mine comes out embarrassingly breathy.

His free hand comes up to brush a strand of hair from my face, and the tenderness in the gesture makes my chest ache. "You know, back to the consent thing," he says softly. "I was awake."

I suck in a painful gulp of air. "Wh-what?"

"Both nights." His thumb traces my cheekbone, his eyes never leaving mine. "Every time you touched me. When your fingers traced my arms, played with my hair." His voice drops even lower. "Every time you whispered my name in the dark, thinking I couldn't hear you."

Heat floods my face as the implications sink in. All those moments I thought were private—my quiet exploration of him, the confessions I breathed into the night… Okay, I might actually die on the spot.

"Why did you let me keep talking?" The words barely make it past my lips.

"Because I wanted to hear everything. Every confession. Every fear." His eyes search mine, stealing my breath. "Every hope."

My heart pounds against my ribs, a desperate rhythm. "And now?"

"Now I want you to say it all again." His thumb traces my bottom lip, igniting every nerve ending. "But this time, looking at me."

23
Holly

The ability to speak slips away with his words and the lazy trail of his thumb seducing my mouth.

Because this is Chance—the man who held my hand in the dark. Who believes in me when I can't believe in myself. The man who hurt me. The man trying so hard to make it right my chest aches.

"I missed you today," he says softly, his thumb still tracing patterns on my skin. "Missed this."

"What, my sparkling wit and casual blackmail?"

"You." The word carries weight, heavy with meaning.

With one small shove, he sits back, looking up at me with heated surprise as I rise to my knees.

"My turn." I plant one knee on either side of his hips, settling into his lap. Because I can't think under him. But up here, I'm in charge. Or at least, it's easier to tell myself that.

His hands automatically grip my waist as I thread my fingers through his hair. "Problem, soldier?"

"Not at all."

I roll my hips experimentally, and his fingers dig into my sides. All that military control, undone by one simple move. An intoxicating rush of power fills me knowing that.

My new favorite game—how many sounds can I drag out of GI Composure before he breaks?

"While I've got you where I want you," I breathe against his ear, "I don't need an assist with living up to the nickname. I'm an overachiever, self-taught, and proven highly proficient."

The sound he makes is absolutely feral. His mouth finds my throat while his hands slide under my sweater and up my spine. But I keep control, using my grip on his hair to guide him where I want him.

Even as my heart threatens to jump straight out of my chest.

Because this is Chance.

The man who's had me hot and bothered since he shamelessly fondled my favorite pair of underwear like some panty bandit.

The one who hurt me.

The one who's trying so hard to make it right that my every cell aches with wanting to take him up on it.

My pulse throbs in my ears. He's so close I can count his eyelashes, see the faint stubble along his jaw.

Also, hello biceps. Those are some grade-A military gains right there.

Focus, Holly. This is not the time to mentally catalog his muscle groups. Even if his forearms should be classified as lethal weapons.

His hand skims up my side, featherlight. "Dangerous game, Squirt."

Oh, we are so far past dangerous. We've blown right through dangerous, made a pit stop at reckless, and are currently speeding toward complete emotional annihilation.

But hey, at least the view is nice.

"I'm not afraid of danger." The words come out breathless.

Apparently, my voice didn't get the memo about playing it cool. Then again, nothing about this is cool. The temperature in here has definitely jumped about twenty degrees, and it's not from the woodstove.

"No." His thumb traces my bottom lip. "You never were. Not *my* Holly."

Maybe it's the way his voice hitches. Maybe it's the way he's looking at me like he'd tear himself apart before hurting me again. Maybe it's just that I'm tired of fighting this thing between us—but the *my Holly*?

Direct hit, soldier.

My Holly.

Two simple words shouldn't be able to crack my chest wide open like this. Shouldn't make my heart flutter and soar and ache all at once.

But they do.

My Holly.

Not William McAdams' disappointing daughter. Not Nick's pesky baby sister. Not the family outcast or a corporate liability.

My Holly.

His. Claimed without hesitation, without conditions or caveats. No need to be quieter, smaller, more polished or proper.

Just… his Holly.

The words settle into my bones, filling cracks I didn't even know were there. Cracks left by every dismissive "dear" and patronizing pat on the head. Every time I was too much or not enough.

But here, with his calloused thumb still tracing my lip like I'm something precious, those two words rewrite everything.

They say "I see you" and "I choose you" and "You're exactly who you're supposed to be" all at once.

I swallow against the tears burning in my throat as the truth of it hits me. No one's ever claimed me like this before. Not as something to be proud of. Not as someone worth keeping, worth fighting for.

Just… mine.

My Holly.

I want to bottle this feeling. Tuck it away somewhere safe where doubt can't touch it. Where I can pull it out on days when I feel invisible and remember that to him, I'm not just Holly.

I'm his Holly.

And maybe that's all I ever needed to be.

His thumb is still on my lip and I'm fighting the urge to bite it. Because that would be crazy, right? Total insanity. Completely unhinged behavior. The kind of thing a normal, rational person definitely wouldn't do...

Unless...

Before I can overthink myself into paralysis, I part my lips just enough to graze his thumb with my teeth.

His pupils dilate, dark eating away at the blue. "Holly." It comes out rough, almost a growl.

Oh.

Oh wow.

That's... that's a sound I'd like to hear again. Preferably on repeat. Maybe as my new ringtone.

"Yes?" I aim for innocent, but it's hard to pull off when you're straddling a wild animal. Or Chance.

His free hand slides into my hair, tilting my head back. "Last chance to tap out."

I actually laugh at that, though it comes out breathier than intended. "Seriously? After all this time, you think I'm backing down now? I literally wrote Christmas porn about your candy cane, Chance. I think we're a little past—"

His mouth crashes into mine, swallowing whatever brilliant thing I was about to say. Probably for the best. I'm pretty sure I was about to make another North Pole joke and—

Oh.

OH.

Never mind. Not thinking anymore. Not doing

anything except feeling his lips on mine, his hands in my hair, and the way he's thrusting his hips into me.

Starting slow, almost careful, he maps my mouth with his. But when I arch into him, fingers curling into his shirt, something snaps.

Harder this time, his mouth devours, like he's trying to memorize my taste. Like he knows what he's about to say. His hands span my rib cage, thumbs brushing just beneath the underwire of my bra, and I shiver.

"When we leave here…" he manages between kisses, and something in his voice traps the air in my lungs.

His hands frame my face, thumbs brushing my cheekbones like I'm something precious. "We can't…"

"Don't." I roll my hips again, swallowing his groan. "Don't ruin this."

He pulls back, resting his forehead against mine. His breathing is as ragged as mine, but there's something else in his eyes. Something that looks terrifyingly like tenderness.

"If I touch you the way I want to touch you, if I look at you like…"

He shakes his head. His hands tighten on my waist. "I won't jeopardize what you're building."

The fierce protectiveness in his voice steals my air far more than any kiss. Because this isn't just about keeping our cover, this is about him putting me first. Putting my dreams first.

"So we'll be professional." I hate how thick my voice sounds, how he can see right through me. "Hands-off policy."

"Hands off," he agrees, though his thumbs are still tracing maddening patterns on my skin like he can't quite make himself stop touching me yet. Like he's trying to memorize how I feel under his hands. "Starting the second we walk out that door. Because you deserve to win this, Holly. You deserve everything."

The way he says it—like it's the simplest truth, like he'd move mountains just to see me succeed—fills me until I'm aching.

A sweet, stunning, torturous sensation of being stitched back together, one frayed piece at a time.

No one has ever believed in me like this. No one's ever looked at me the way he is right now, like I'm simultaneously the strongest and most precious thing he's ever seen.

"Everything?" I whisper, hating how vulnerable I sound.

"Everything." He catches my chin, making sure I meet his eyes. "And I'll spend however long it takes proving that to you. Starting with watching you crush this presentation."

I lean in, pressing my forehead to his. "Even if it means pretending you hate me?"

"Even then." His voice roughens. "Though for the record? Hardest damn act I've ever had to pull off."

"Thank you." The word is barely a whisper. Probably the quietest I've ever been in my life.

"You're welcome." He punctuates the word with a gentle kiss to the corner of my mouth, just like the one that devastated me in all the best ways, only on the opposite side.

"Let me ask you something?" His thumb traces my bottom lip again. Like he can't stop going back to continue that barest touch—his touch so gentle it makes my chest ache.

"What's that?" The word comes out breathier than I intend.

"This thing with your dad's company—is it about running it or proving you're more than his little…" He winces. "…princess?"

My heart stutters.

Trust Chance to see right through my armor, past all my carefully constructed plans, straight to the tender spots I try to keep hidden.

"Maybe both?"

"You're already more, Holly." His voice drops low, intimate. "Anyone with eyes can see it. But building a life around proving it to someone who might never see you the way you deserve? That's not the Holly I know."

Something in me cracks wide open. "So what then —just give up? Let him win?"

"No." His fingers thread through my hair, cradling my head. "Build your own empire. One where no one can question if you earned it. One where you don't have to fight for a seat at his table. One where once you get that seat, you don't have to spend every day after continuing to prove you deserve to be there."

The possibility hits me like a shot of pure adrenaline

—no more trying to fit into the box my father built. No more measuring myself against his expectations.

Just… freedom.

"That sounds…" Terrifying. Exhilarating. Like standing on the edge of a black diamond run, heart racing, knowing the only way down is to jump.

"Like you." He gives me a reassuring smile. "The Holly who's never met a challenge she couldn't crush."

And just like that, we're back to us.

Different, deeper, but still us.

The rest can wait until after I win.

24
CHANCE

EVE
Mayday!

EVE
Mayday!

EVE
This is not a drill.

EVE
All hands on deck.

ME
What the hell did you do?

EVE
I may have overseasoned the steak, if you know what I mean

CHARLIE
Actually, I don't know what that means

EVE

I promised to loosen up the 'rents, did I
not?

HOLLY

I sense a go big or go home situation
here.

NICK

Shit.

EVE

It was fine. Going great. Smooth as silk.
Everything ship shape.

CHARLIE

We've heard this before

ME

Where the hell are you? The first rule in a
rescue mission... COORDINATES!

EVE

Great room. Too close to the bar

HOLLY

Meaning???

EVE

Meaning I might have been too generous
spiking the 'ole nog

NICK

I have kiss trauma. Is whatever I'm
walking to going to add to that?

HOLLY

I feel safe saying yes

EVE

Man, I Feel Like A Woman just started
and I underestimated my powers.
HURRY!

ME

We're almost there

NICK

Who's we?

HOLLY

UH

EVE

You didn't tell him???

NICK

Tell me what?

EVE

That Holly's been connecting to
Chance's super-secret network.

NICK

Now what the hell does that mean? Give
it to me in slots

ME

Nick my man, did you just make a joke?

NICK

It was an accident.

ME

I'm a proud papa anyway. My boy got
his big boy hairs.

Social hour in full swing.

Yup.

Traumatizing karaoke stealing the show.

Double yup.

And Holly? Well, she's out here trying to finish me off entirely, strolling into the room like some kind of Christmas temptation wrapped in nothing but a sweater and those socks—red and white stripes hugging her calves, looking like they were spun straight out of Santa's wet dream.

Only, this candy cane isn't hanging on *my* tree where it belongs. Nope. She's put herself right on display for the communal tree.

Like that's okay.

As if I didn't come down ahead of her to give her a chance to change.

Like it's fine for every set of eyes in this room to be dragging over what's mine.

I pocket my phone and survey the scene. A muscle ticks in my jaw. Something that seems to happen a lot lately.

I've hacked computer systems in active war zones that were less daunting than this—the raw chaos of family, holiday cheer, and Holly's thigh-high sneak attack in full force.

The worst part? The way those socks are drawing more than a few lingering, interested looks.

Each one like a goddamn challenge.

Too bad for them, I don't play fair. And I don't share.

Looks like I'll be handing out some festive injuries. Merry slasher Christmas, assholes.

"Man! I Feel Like a Woman" blares through the lodge's great room speakers, the chorus becoming the battle cry of my mother's latest holiday war crime. Her off-key rendition is loud enough to startle the wildlife outside, and she wields an empty wine bottle like it's a Grammy.

This is the same woman who once gave me a two-hour lecture on proper dinner etiquette before my first formal. Now, she's strutting across the room like she's possessed by Shania Twain, throwing in a shoulder shimmy that would make the devil himself ask for a time-out.

"Let's go, girls!" she belts out, shimmying right toward my father, who is definitely loosening his tie with far too much enthusiasm. If this is leading to some kind of striptease duet, I'm going to need a support group. I've seen combat horrors that haunt me, but this?

This should not be the cure to lingering PTSD.

Holly leans in close, her breath warm against my ear, her voice low and full of amusement that's doing things to me it shouldn't.

Not with her brother watching.

"Remember when you said you'd rather face enemy combatants than deal with family drama?"

"Yeah?" My voice comes out rougher than I intend because she's right there. Close enough that I catch her scent, warm and sweet and so uniquely Holly. Something I directly associate with late nights, her curled against me, and confessions.

It's a direct attack on my ability to concentrate.

"I think the enemy just called for backup."

Sure enough, our mothers are in full duet mode now, attempting choreography that makes them look like they're leading a Zumba class on a sinking ship.

Mrs. McAdams' once-pristine hair is coming undone, strands sticking out like she's one wrong move away from starring in a holiday horror flick.

She goes for a spin—bold choice considering the eggnog levels in her bloodstream—and wobbles dangerously close to the Christmas wishing tree. My instincts kick in, but Holly's hand clamps on to my arm, stopping me in my tracks.

"Should we…" She gestures vaguely at the unfolding disaster, her fingers sliding down my arm to curl around my bicep. I'm suddenly hyperaware of every point of contact—every warm inch of her skin against mine— and Nick's laser-beam stare burning into my side.

"Interfere with a direct order from Command? Not a chance," I reply, forcing myself to take a sip of whiskey and, in the process, casually break her grip under her brother's watchful glare.

For the best, especially since her sweater has slipped off her shoulder again, revealing just enough skin to make me reconsider my entire moral code.

"Besides," I add, nodding toward the chaos because it's a hell of a lot safer than looking at her with Nick's words running through my head on a loop, "your mom just saved that spin with remarkable agility for someone who's had that much rum."

Give it to me in slots.

And there is your answer, my dude. I'm going to give it to your sister in all of her slots.

Repeatedly.

For… oh, let's say at least the next fifty or sixty years.

Hell, it's going to be my new business venture.

Retire from the Army and put my skills to work making Holly the single most satisfied CEO in the history of CEOs.

My business plan is solid, on brand, and there's no way I can lose.

Man on the ground, doing the dirty work.

Horny. Dirty. Work.

Stick with what you know. Utilize your skills.

After corporate hours I'll fill her slots until she's a sobbing, gasping, squirting mess.

During corporate hours, your CEO fills *your* slots in record-setting abundance.

Free childcare?

Slot check.

Zero deductible health insurance company-wide?

Slot check.

Guaranteed bonuses?

You bet your sweet ass… slot fucking check!

And since I'm a pro at taking care of *her* sweet ass, she's going to rain them on you like the candyman… starting with quarterly.

I might be onto something here. The answer to world peace? Penetrate CEOs across the board.

Deliver a virus to the system that infiltrates with one hundred percent precision, ultimately delivering exponential employee satisfaction.

Companies, communities, and finally, the world.

Jesus Christ.

I'm. Fucking. Losing. It.

She presents tomorrow morning. I just have to hold it together for one more day.

But with Holly in those socks and that damn sweater? I'm pretty sure tomorrow's going to finish what today started.

"The best part of being a woman!" my mother belts out, punctuating each syllable with a hip thrust so aggressive it drags me out of all of Holly's slots.

Nick materializes at my shoulder, his expression one step shy of shell shock.

I guess it's better than the burning glare. You know, if we weren't both in serious danger of never sporting wood again.

He gestures to the horror show unfolding. "We need to shut this down before—"

"The clothes are coming off!" My dad announces, already halfway through unbuttoning his shirt.

"—that happens," Nick finishes, his tone grim.

Eve pops up like an enthusiastic chaos gremlin, phone raised and already recording. "Oh no, this is content, a case study in overshooting my mark."

"For posterity?" I mutter, trying to make sense of her

enthusiasm in light of the mistletoe kiss gone sideways trauma she's been wrestling with.

"Blackmail," Eve supplies, flashing a grin that's purely predatory.

Charlie shrugs, utterly unbothered. "Solid evidence that they are actually human." She nudges Eve's elbow. "Send me a copy."

Before I can intervene, Holly plucks Charlie's phone right out of her hands. "Nope. Some things shouldn't outlive the moment." Her fingers brush mine as she passes me the phone for safekeeping. It's barely a second of contact, but it might as well be a live wire straight to my nervous system.

And then, like the harbinger of doom, the opening notes of "Suspicious Minds" blare through the lodge's speakers. My father steps up, tie already gone, shirt hanging open, and—oh God—is he trying to swivel his hips like Elvis?

God, this should be on National Geographic.

"Watch as the patriarchs engage in what appears to be an Elvis-inspired dominance display. The loosening of neckties indicates escalating testosterone levels..." Eve begins as though she plucked the thought right out of my head and ran with it.

"Move in," I growl at Nick. "Standard extraction protocol."

He nods, grim and resigned. "You take point on your dad, I'll handle mine?"

"Wait!" Holly's hand grabs my arm again, grounding me in a way that has absolutely no place in a family karaoke nightmare. "Give me a minute. I have an idea."

She vanishes into the crowd that's now forming a semicircle around our fathers, who are dangerously close to making "Suspicious Minds" live up to its name.

"The pack seems to be fueled by a potent combination of eggnog and repressed suburban impulses. Scientists remain baffled by this phenomenon," Eve goes on, making me wonder if she didn't suck down a bit of the nog from hell herself.

Nick stares at her, his expression a strange cocktail of horror and morbid fascination, like he's watching a train wreck he secretly hopes will derail into another. "You're disturbingly good at that."

Just seconds later, as Dad hits what can only be described as a lethal hip roll channeling Elvis himself, the karaoke track cuts out, replaced by the unmistakable opening bars of "Sweet Caroline."

The reaction is instant and almost Pavlovian. Our parents freeze mid-performance before bursting into delighted cheers. In seconds, they're swaying arm in arm, their previous antics forgotten in the glow of collegiate nostalgia.

"Genius," Nick breathes, clearly awed by the strategic brilliance of the move.

"Pure evil genius," I correct, my lips twitching as I watch Holly, smug as hell. That flirty little hop step keeps her sweater slipping off her shoulder, revealing just enough golden skin to make me forget we're surrounded by witnesses.

"Get a room," Charlie mutters as she brushes past.

"We have one," Holly fires back, her timing too perfect for comfort. "But someone's mother keeps organizing family activities."

I choke on my whiskey, torn between pride at her quick wit and panic as Nick's head turns with analyst precision.

"We?"

"Supersecret network purposes only," I croak, but I'm already calculating how many more slips we can afford before Nick puts it together.

25
CHANCE

It's taking every last shred of my self-control not to cross this room, toss her over my shoulder, and march off like a caveman. Straight to her soft, warm bed where the first thing I'm going to do is give her the fucking kiss her pussy begged me for when she had me locked between the socks.

Just one more night… Just one more night… Just one more night…

My motto, my mantra, my battle cry—whatever you want to call it, is reduced to those four words.

They're my white-knuckle grip on my dwindling reason.

This time tomorrow, she and I will put the energy pulsing through both of us to good work.

Just one more night of my cock throbbing incessantly, leaving me grinding my fucking sheets like a ten-year-old starring in REMageddon: The Final Spurt. A race to nut before the sunrise.

Okay, seriously, I need her to go to her room. I can't. This is more than a medical condition at this point. It's medical, psychological, and behavioral.

I pull out my phone, my fingers flying over the screen.

ME

Those socks are a security breach, Squirt.

HOLLY

Didn't know you were the sock police, soldier boy. What's wrong with my socks? 😐

ME

You know exactly what's wrong with them. Those are MY socks. MY thighs 🔥🔥

HOLLY

Funny, I don't see your name on them. Now Otis, on the other hand 😏

ME

Keep it up, Squirt. You're gonna pay for this later 😈

HOLLY

Gee... what are you going to do? Lay beside me again tonight and touch me exactly... nowhere 🙄

Yeah, nowhere.

Because the moment I touch her like that, it's game on—and we both know I'm not equipped for half-measures.

I drag my gaze away from her legs—a herculean feat—and catch sight of Everett's uncle Seth at the end of the bar.

His hair's a touch grayer than I remember, but that's where time stopped bothering with him.

Firmly planted in that mid-generation sweet spot—old enough to be respectable, young enough to still get away with questionable decisions. He was our unofficial booze supplier, thanks to that perfect balance of "cool uncle" energy and "don't ask, don't tell" policies.

When his gaze catches mine, recognition lights up his face. His smile stretches wider, and he nods, raising his beer in a silent, easygoing salute.

"When did your uncle get back?" I ask, returning my focus to Everett drying high-ball glasses with the practiced ease he learned in the years following college—his nomad years—otherwise known as the running from Sierra years.

"A month or so ago, about the time my dad announced he's permanently handing me the keys to the kingdom."

I glance at his uncle, now laughing with Cleo at the end of the bar. "And he's… cool with that?"

"Why wouldn't he be? He's never been interested in running the place but likes to stay busy, so with Aunt Rosie gone, he's helping me renovate. Keeps him out of trouble."

"Wait—where's Aunt Rosie? She didn't…"

"Die?" Everett barks out a laugh. "No. Let's just say

whatever happened was mutual. He won't spill, but judging by the way he's working through every available skirt in this town, he's more than fine."

"Ah, a true Morgan recovery plan." I smirk. "They teach that alongside ski lessons or what?"

"Pretty much. I'd like to think it's genetic. I bet you're glad you left your skirt at home, aren't ya?"

He gives me a fucking wink meant for—anyone but me. Must need the practice since it's the same one he uses to charm women straight out of their clothes after he uses my moves to get them to his room.

Funny how just two days ago, I was ready to brutally murder him for those.

Now I just want to smack him around a little, big brother style.

"Yeah, not sure I can handle your uncle Seth. You remember that New Year's party the year after we graduated? He gave me some advice about what ladies want. I know way too much about your aunt Rosie now."

Everett immediately throws a hand up, signaling me to shut the hell up. "Nope. Nope. Not doing this. I already need therapy for the summer I helped her clean out her closet and found her vibrator stash. Now you want to mix that into my mental soup? Hard pass."

"Now those images are mixing in mine. Appreciate it," I say with a pained laugh before taking another sip of my drink.

"I've gotta say, man, night and day difference between you now and a few years ago when you came up to lick your wounds."

"Doesn't take much to look better than the pile of shit I looked like when I cruised into town then." I'd finally found out the extent of my ex-wife's cheating and filed for divorce. I knew I was on borrowed time to tell my parents before they found out on their own.

I wouldn't let that happen. I wouldn't let my father try to reduce me to some dumb kid who hid from the truth and responsibility.

But first, a bender so fucked up it carried a significant risk of death and altered my brain chemistry.

Actually…

I steal a glance out of the corner of my eye at my current *bender* where she throws back her head in laughter at something Eve says. The line of her jaw where it meets the shallow valley of her neck just begs for my mouth.

Her head tilts just so…

Yup, that's the spot right there.

Definitely fucked.

Significant risk of death by big bro rage or lock cock.

That's a thing, right?

And for-fucking-sure, it's altered my brain chemistry.

Everett hums, that knowing fucking hum of his, as his gaze flicks toward Holly. "I mean, I'm not saying it's her or anything…"

I stop my glass halfway to my mouth and pin him with a mind-your-own-damn-business glare.

Yeah, not going to admit it, guy.

When I finally confess, there's only one man I owe the truth to… and an apology.

"Sure, right about the time you finally admit that you and Sierra have unfinished business." I toss back the rest of my drink after dropping the bomb. That should wipe the smirk off his face.

Everett's smile slips for a short, unsatisfying second before he slaps it back into place and lies to us both. "No unfinished business. She made her choices."

"So that's it. They're written in stone, then? By that logic, I'd still be with Noelle."

He shrugs. "Marriages on paper are a thing."

"Bite your fucking tongue clean off, asshole." He knows firsthand how fucked up I was during that time.

Apparently, my barb hit harder than he wanted to admit, but still—fuck.

It all goes away tomorrow because the truth will be out. But for him, who knows how long he and Sierra will do this dance.

I'm definitely giving him back the shit he likes to dish out.

Everett laughs and tosses the towel over his shoulder. "Oooh, testy tonight. Well then, you aren't going to want to turn around."

"Yeah, why's th—"

The words die on my tongue when I turn to Holly and find Everett's uncle strolling over, casual as can be, but for the inferno of interest in his eyes.

Interest locked on Holly where she's perched on the window seat, her legs tucked under her, glowing under the twinkling lights sweeping across the window as she laughs at something Eve says.

Fucking dick-swinging Morgan men.

"She's got a target painted on her forehead," Everett says lightly. "Or, you know, her lips."

Every muscle in my shoulders locks.

Son of a bitch!

About five feet above her and partially obscured by the string lights—the goddamn mistletoe hanging like a fucking omen.

"My uncle has excellent aim. You gonna stand here and let him take his shot, or are you gonna handle that?"

I snag my phone from my pocket and bring up my gallery.

Yup, there it is, right at the top.

Time-stamped two hours and fourteen minutes ago. The mistletoe over the entry to the great room.

Because this is what I've been reduced to.

Tracking a mistletoe.

Collecting evidence.

Glancing up at the exact area now, and… no mistletoe. "The fuck?"

Slamming my glass down, I slide off the stool when something catches my attention from my peripherals.

A tool belt propped along the wall at the end of the bar.

The hammer.

Oh, I'll handle it.

Curling my hand around the handle, I flash back to the way Holly gripped this very fucking hammer from the looks and set everyone straight.

Most of all me.

Yeah, this would do. This would fucking do nicely.

I test the weight, adjust my grip, and tear up the distance between me and the goddamn problem.

By the time Seth leans into her—too fucking close and too fucking charming—with his hand braced against the ledge next to her head, I'm there.

Barely registering Holly's widened eyes, I slide between her and Everett's uncle, keeping her tucked firmly behind me.

Uncle Seth's grin widens, and I'm moving before I can stop myself, my face stopping just inches in front of him.

"Chance? What are you—"

"No." It's low and rough—a demand, a declaration —a single-syllable warning in a tone conveying any number of nightmare scenarios for Uncle Seth's untimely death. "She's taken."

Seth's grin widens, his hands raised in mock surrender. "Easy there, Chance. Just thought I'd do my part. You know, tradition and all that."

I narrow my eyes at him, my jaw clenching until my teeth ache. "Find another tradition."

He chuckles, unbothered. "If you say so." Leaning around me, he tips an imaginary hat to Holly. "Ma'am."

Slick motherfucker.

"What the hell are you doing?" she demands—her voice low, but sharp—all while delivering a hell of a poke to my goddamn kidney.

She's trying to sound indignant, but there's something else beneath it. Something that sounds a lot like excitement.

"What I should've done after the first damn time." I spin on her and prop my hand in the same spot Everett's uncle had.

Each word is a growl fueled by frustration, pining, lust, and fucking restraint choking me since I walked into that fucking airport and found her on her knees with her ass in the air.

"Yeah, soldier boy… and what's that?" Her eyes gleam and her lips twitch, right where I kissed her at the bonfire.

Oh, she knows exactly what she's doing.

In two steps, I'm looming over her, a boot planted on the bench on either side of her hips.

Eve says something, probably another play-by-play, but I can't distinguish a word, not with the adrenaline surging through me and the deafening pounding of my heart.

This wasn't an accident.

It was a goddamn masterpiece of self-sabotage.

This angle leaves her mouthwatering throat exposed and stretched tight.

Fire and barely banked lust simmer in her eyes.

Only overshadowed by raw hunger when her gaze sweeps over my cock, straining against the cargos she's in a love-hate relationship with.

"Room. Now."

She glares up at me, her jaw set in fierce defiance. "You're not the boss of me."

"You better run, Squirt." Raising the hammer, I swing and hook the claw around the nailhead with every bit of violence simmering inside from endless days subjected to various forms of torture.

Every form beginning and ending with the same ingredient: Holly fucking McAdams.

Wood splinters.

The hammer catches on the string lights, ripping a series of hooks off the window frame, leaving them drooping in Holly and Eve's laps.

Our gazes lock.

She's all fluttering breaths, pretty little mouth hanging open with shock to my chest heaving, jaw tight, teeth gnashing in frustration that's finally reached its boiling point.

She blinks and whatever showdown we're locked in ends.

Wonder who won?

She's shooting off the bench the very next second, but I'm not fooling myself that she's all of a sudden willing to follow orders.

Not at all.

Somehow, her retreat serves a purpose, and I'm about to find out what that purpose is.

The sense of reason I pride myself on surrenders to reckless energy that's out of bounds, beyond reason, and completely unstoppable.

With a yank fueled by a week's worth of being edged by the evil little bastard swinging overhead, I rip the nail clean out of the wood, dragging the mistletoe down with it.

No more pictures to document where this little fucker is.

No more wondering when the next temptation will be shoved in my face.

No more questions from Nick when I kiss her in front of him again.

No. Fucking. More.

Heading for her room, I take the stairs two at a time, hammer clenched in one hand and the mistletoe swinging from my fist in the other.

I throw open her door with a force fueled by blue balls, the ache in my cock unbearable. The sharp crack of wood crashing into the wall is a brutal punctuation as if the room itself is bracing for what's coming.

We're about to test the limits of damage deposits.

Buckle the fuck up.

26
CHANCE

The door slams with enough force to rattle the frame, my hands shaking as I throw the lock and chain into place. Everything inside me coils tight, muscles wound to the breaking point after a week of holding back.

Holly kneels on the bed, all flushed cheeks and heaving chest, looking at me like she knows exactly what she's done.

What she's been doing to me—piece by fucking piece—with those socks, her endless supply of sweaters, and every goddamn smirk.

"The mistletoe wins." The words rasp out of my throat, rough and ragged, worn thin by a week of suppressed need.

"It's got legs." One step closer, my blood pounds in rhythm with every word.

"It's got wings."

She drags her teeth over that full bottom lip, and the sight hits me like a physical blow.

"It's got a fucking twin." Another step. The mattress dips as I plant my hands on either side of her, caging her in, every nerve in my body coiled and ready to snap.

"It's got me kissing your fucking brother."

The words rip out of me, sharp and raw, frustration and hunger colliding so violently I feel like I might burst apart if I don't do something—anything—to make this stop.

And while I'm falling apart?

Her bow-shaped mouth gives way to a smirk of pure pleasure.

Like my sanity shattering is a Broadway show for her fucking entertainment.

And then she laughs.

The breathless, flirty laugh that tells you she's up to something.

That wicked little laugh of hers sparks something primal in me.

I dive my fingers into her hair—rough, without finesse—the mistletoe tangling in her waves. The force enough to yank her head back and tear a surprised gasp from her mouth.

The air between us is charged with every feeling we've battled—temptation, frustration, jealousy, and raw need so overwhelming it's drowning us both.

Me faster than her.

But if I go down, I'm dragging her with me.

Her blown pupils and eyelids heavy with lust draw me in deeper.

Always deeper with her.

A split second later, I claim her mouth—rough, desperate, and everything I've been craving.

Possessive, deep, and demanding—it's angry with every brutal swipe of my tongue—payback for stealing me out of the safety I'd so carefully built.

It's my turn now.

I hook my forearms under her thighs and slam her back onto the mattress, swallowing her breathless gasp. Her knees cage my hips, and my cock finds home against her heat—fuck if it isn't perfect.

Like she was made for this.

For me.

Those blazing, hungry eyes lock on mine reaching straight past my defenses to touch parts of me I've kept locked away.

Rising over her, I position the nail against the headboard right over her head. "This kinky fucker likes to watch? Fine, he gets the best seat in the house."

The nail gleams in the lamplight, mocking me one last time before the crack of the hammer drives it into the wood. Each strike echoes in time with the pulse pounding in my skull.

With one final blow from the side, the nail surrenders and folds, trapping that manipulative little sprig in place.

"Let's see the little fucker move now," I declare, hooking the claw of the hammer over the headboard, leaving the handle jutting out like a warning over what's mine.

The mistletoe might be ahead, but I have a point on the scoreboard now.

A smirk tugs at my mouth as I enjoy the sight of Holly slack-jawed and speechless beneath me.

"Now I've got you right where I want you…" I nudge her mouth closed with my knuckle. A damn shame because I know exactly how to put that mouth to use—but we've got time.

"…under my hammer."

"Oh my God, you've lost your fucking mind." Her voice trembles with surprise and something darker, something that matches the inferno raging under my skin.

My hands find her thighs, where impossibly soft skin meets the top edge of the damn socks that have been torturing me all week. My fingertips sink into her flesh with my possessive grip—*mine.*

"Or I've finally found it." The words come out quiet and reverent because this feels like more than victory.

It feels like coming home.

Her palm settles over my hand—a simple touch, but it sends electricity crackling through my veins, alive and undeniable.

How she says my name—soft and wanting—nearly breaks me.

The glint of her glasses on the nightstand catches my eye. Snagging the delicate gold frames, I bring them to her face and slide them on with deliberate care, making sure they're perfectly in place.

"Glasses on when I'm fucking you," I command, my voice thick with lust.

She sucks in a breath, her lips trembling.

My fingers drag over the strip of bare skin where her thigh meets the edge of her panties. That goddamn spot —that one that's been haunting me every night when she throws a leg over me in her sleep. The same place I took in the sleigh.

It's forbidden, and it's been calling to me ever since, daring me to lose control.

She responds instantly, knees falling open, inviting me in. When my hand slides beneath her sweater, her skin sears against my palm, leaving another mark on me.

My weakness all week—now she's here, spread out before me like a feast, and I plan to devour every inch.

"Chance…" she moans my name, a husky plea and a challenge all at once.

"Shhhhh, no talking when the ride's in motion. Isn't that the rule?" I drag my teeth along her inner thigh, making her gasp.

"Funny, I remember quite a few rules—oh fuck—" Her voice breaks on a low groan as I bite down gently.

My jagged breaths turn shallow as I hook my finger under the edge of her panties and drag them aside. The sight of her steals what's left of my self-control—slick, perfect, and mine for the taking.

Mine.

I give her one last grin. She doesn't shy away or

hide. No, not my Holly. She stares straight at me from the haze of lust—transfixed.

The last thing I see is her eyes rolling back as I disappear from her view. Running my tongue along her slit, I savor her sweetness, the way her body trembles beneath me while circling her clit with the tip of my tongue.

Teasing her flesh, I draw out her pleasure until she's writhing and gasping.

"Fuck, Chance, I need—I," she chokes on simple words, thrashing under my mouth as though she can get away from me—as though she can save herself—from our absolute destruction.

"What was that, baby?" I circle her clit slowly as her jagged pants fill the air. "Can't hear you over how fucking wet you are for me."

She tries to grind against my face, but I pin her hips down. "Chance, please…"

"Mmmm, so bossy one minute, but begging the next. Please, what?" I slip one finger inside her, groaning at how tight she is. "Tell me what you need."

"Need you to stop being such a fucking tease and make me come."

I add another finger, curling them just right. "After the week you put me through? The socks. The sweaters. The Ring Pops. *My fucking shirt.*" I pick up the pace. "I don't think so, Squirt. You're going to earn it."

Her back arches off the bed with a growl in her throat. "I hate you."

"That's okay, you go ahead and hate me. Because your pussy doesn't." I press my tongue flat against her clit. "Feel how she's gripping my fingers? So desperate for it."

"Fuck," panting, she writhes under me. Wild and chaotic, every muscle pulls taut. Her sounds grow more frantic and desperate as she chases her release.

Sweat dots her skin as her gasps turn into tortured groans.

Look at you climb, baby.

"That's it, let me hear you." I suck her clit between my lips. "Show me how much you love my mouth on your pussy."

Curling my fingers deeper, I add pressure in just the right spot that has her twisting away from the pleasure.

She can fight it; she can rail against losing control, but she'll never stop it.

She sucks in a harsh breath, the air skidding to a clean stop deep in her lungs. Her back bows helplessly under the onslaught of tension.

And when that breath finally releases, her hips buck against my face, and the scream tears through her, barely muffled by the pillow she's biting.

A victim to her own body now, I don't let her ride it out and come down.

Fuck that.

I haven't come down once from what she's been doing to me this week—every look, every touch, every tease driving me closer to the edge.

I don't need any help living up to the nickname...

That's what she said.

Too bad—she's getting help anyway.

I unleash a frenzy on her clit with the pads of my fingers, jerking side to side relentlessly, until she snaps.

She comes hard, my name a broken cry ripped from her lips, soaking my face, my tongue, and the sheets beneath her as I work her through it.

I stay on her as she falls apart, pulling every broken whimper from her until she's trembling, wrecked, and a mess beneath me.

When her breathing slows, her chest still heaving, and her skin flushed to perfection, I crawl up her body and crush my mouth to hers, letting her taste herself slick and hot on my lips.

Sucking my tongue hard, all filthy and desperate, like she can't get enough, only fuels me to ruin her all over again.

"Mmmmm," I growl against her lips. "Getting off on tasting yourself on my tongue."

She nips my bottom lip. "Just wait until I taste your cock on my tongue."

Fuck.

I pull back, locking my gaze on hers, my grin sharp. "We're just getting started. My mission? Carve our initials inside you, stroke by relentless stroke. Think you'll survive?"

Her eyes darken with desire, and she smirks right back at me. "Bring it on, soldier boy."

27
Holly

Chance devours me with greedy eyes as we tear away what little clothing we have left. His gaze burns into my skin as I stand before him in only my thigh-high socks and glasses.

Three seconds. That's all it takes—then he's on me. His mouth slants hot and desperate over mine, his fingers tangling in my hair like he's afraid to let go. With his body pressing into me and his kiss swallowing me whole, all I can do is hold on for dear life.

Muscles roll and flex under my hands as he marches me backward, step by deliberate step until my knees hit the edge of the bed.

A low, dark groan rumbles from his chest, vibrating into my mouth when my nails scrape lightly over his skin, teasing him just enough to feel his restraint fray.

He doesn't just crawl over me—he stalks me like

prey, deliberate and unrelenting, until he's exactly where he belongs, nestled between my legs.

His strong hand clamps possessively on my hip. With a dominant tug, he drags me onto his thighs like he can't stand even a sliver of space between us.

Looming over me, his shadow stealing my breath, and all I can do is marvel at him. I barely register the sound of him tearing open a condom. By the time I realize he protected us both, he's already reaching for the hammer hooked over the headboard, claiming it like a vow.

Soldier boy is bringing the hammer from now on, because this?

This is the single hottest thing I've ever seen.

His forearm flexes as he adjusts his grip—his body taut with restrained power—the head of his cock brushing my entrance, teasing me with every deliberate move.

I look up at him, my heart pounding so hard it feels like it might crack my ribs. For all his intensity, it's the tenderness in his eyes that renders me stupidly silent— the unspoken promise that this moment isn't just about his pleasure but about us.

"Ready, baby?" he murmurs, his voice rough, the rasp sending shivers straight down my spine. His thumb drags over my bottom lip, slow and deliberate, a tease and a question all in one.

"Do your worst, soldier boy." I sink my teeth into the pad of his thumb, and his pupils blow wide. Raw hunger flashes through his gaze so fiercely, I'm transfixed.

Hips surging forward, he drives his cock into me with one hard, definitive thrust.

Pleasure teeters on the edge of pain, the explosion deep and all-consuming. Thick and heavy, he forces me to accommodate every inch, as he channels a week's worth of frustration and restraint into punishment so hot it sends me reeling.

My gasps come wild and ragged making my throat ache while his every punishing thrust delivers that perfect, mind-shattering stretch and fullness.

There's no room to adjust—no reprieve, only him. He withdraws almost completely, only to slam back into me, the hammer a taut anchor in his grip. His rhythm—a rolling plunge and drag, retreating just enough to pull me apart all over again. My hands fly to his shoulders, nails biting into his skin as he takes everything with ruthless, possessive strokes.

Closer.

I need to be closer.

All the places he loves to claim on me—behind my ear, along my throat, the ridge of my shoulders—they call to me now, begging to be marked in return.

Hooking my hands behind his neck, I pull myself up to him, meeting him heartbeat to heartbeat, my breasts pressed to his solid frame. Every brush of my nipples against the dusting of hair on his skin sends sharp jolts of heat straight through me.

But it's not enough.

When he tightens his arm around me, pulling me closer with a low, primal growl, it still isn't enough.

My hand snakes over the back of his head, up to where the hair is a tad longer on top. I give it a tug, dragging his head back, and lean in, grazing the sensitive spot just behind his ear.

He jerks, his arm squeezing tight, and a shudder rips through him into me.

Harder. Wilder.

Oh—oh. I—wow.

I trail my tongue along the column of his throat, over the bob of his Adam's apple, licking my way to the underside of his jaw.

His jagged groan vibrates against my lips, spurring me on.

His thrusts grow more erratic, each one hitting harder, rougher. The power of driving him to this point, of unraveling him completely, only makes me want to push him further over the edge.

Clinging to him, the salt of his skin still heavy on my tongue, I sink my teeth into the ridge of his shoulder, desperate to anchor myself.

He jerks, a ragged groan ripping from his chest as his hips slam into me.

"Fuck, Holly," he snarls, his hand digging into my hip. His movements turn erratic, each thrust harder than the last. He fucks me like I'm a vendetta, and this is the final showdown.

I choke on the gasp tearing from my throat and claw at his back. I'll never be the same—not when every brutal thrust feels like he's tearing me apart and reshaping me from the inside out.

Not when the raw, unfiltered need in his eyes burns through me, stripping away everything I thought I knew about sex and intimacy. Rewriting it all with him at the center.

The sound of flesh meeting flesh echoes, loud and primal, pulling me under. Wrapping my legs around his waist, I dig my heels into his taut ass, urging him deeper, needing more, all of him.

The pressure coiling inside me winds tighter and tighter with every relentless stroke, every driving thrust. His mouth finds mine, hot and desperate, his kiss as consuming as the way he moves inside me.

When he finally abandons my swollen lips, his mouth devours my throat, trailing heat down to my collarbone, leaving me gasping.

His hands roam to my breasts, his mouth finding one nipple, sucking it into the wet heat of his mouth. The drag of his teeth sends a shock straight through me, and just as I'm about to lose myself in the teasing pleasure, he surges into me again.

Hard. Demanding. Relentless.

And fuck me, I want it all.

Despite his iron grip on the hammer, the headboard bangs against the wall with each powerful surge. The more he looks into my eyes, the more erratic his movements become until the composed, regimented GI Joe I've always known dissolves into a man consumed.

All guttural snarls and fractured control, he's the most beautiful thing I've ever seen.

"You're mine," he growls, the possessive claim making my walls clench hard around him.

"I'm gonna ruin you for any other man. This pussy, the socks, Otis—" His hand skims the valley between my breasts, coming to rest over my racing heart, his eyes blazing. "And this? It all belongs to me."

His dominance, his sheer intensity—it's too much. It crashes over me in waves, and I tumble over the edge with a cry, my vision whiting out as pleasure takes me.

Each pulse of release expands and consumes, leaving me wrecked and growing all at once.

There's no recovering from this fall. There's only Chance—relentless, keeping me suspended in this place of reeling, unending pleasure.

Even as he takes me with a ferocity that leaves me gasping for air, his touches are threaded with love. The way his fingers brush a stray lock of hair from my face, lingering against my cheek. The soft kisses he presses to my neck, my collarbone, my lips, reverent even as his pace drives me wild.

"So beautiful, my Holly," he murmurs.

I whimper as he hits that perfect spot inside me, over and over, the pressure swelling, throbbing, dancing on the edge of pain. Sparks shoot through me, curling my toes and leaving me clinging to him like he's the only thing keeping me from shattering completely.

He growls, his grip on the hammer tightening as his thrusts grow rougher, more desperate, each one chasing the release we both need. "Let go, baby," he rasps, his hand cupping my chin as he leans in, his voice a low, sinful command. "Choke my cock with that boss bitch pussy of yours one more time."

And then I'm gone. Tumbling, spiraling, breaking as my orgasm consumes me completely, unapologetically. My vision blurs, my body shakes, and waves of unrelenting pleasure flood every nerve, making me cry out his name.

I can't tear my eyes from his as it happens—watching him watch me, his gaze full of raw, animalistic satisfaction as I fall apart around him.

Until his jaw goes slack, his body jerks, and with a ferocious, guttural shout, he follows me over the edge. His cock pulses inside me, and I feel him give me every piece of himself, no holding back, no restraint.

We collapse together, our bodies slick with sweat, our hearts pounding in sync like they've always meant to be this way. He gathers me close, his arms strong and warm, holding me like he never intends to let go.

As I catch my breath, my cheek resting against his chest, I know—this is it. Right here, in his arms, is exactly where I'm meant to be.

28

Holly

Every delicious ache in my body reminds me of last night—his mouth, his hands, the way he made me beg while gripping that hammer like it was the only anchor in a storm neither of us could escape.

My thighs quiver with each step, tiny aftershocks of pleasure rippling through me. Each one a replay of him claiming every inch of my body.

Staring into my reflection, towel tucked around me, I search for the version of myself I need to be to make my father see what everyone else already has.

"You know that towel isn't bulletproof, right?" Chance's voice carries that gravelly edge that makes the most sensitive parts of me flare to life. "Pretty sure staring it down won't make it stop attacking your confidence."

My lips twitch. I adjust the towel, dragging it up a bit higher until Otis peeks out from beneath the terrycloth. "The view's not bad, though. Care to weigh in, soldier boy?"

His jaw ticks—once, twice. His eyes rake over me like I'm his next mission objective. Good. After what he did to me last night, *turnabout's* fair play.

He dangles my favorite panties between his fingers. "Special delivery."

My favorite Fall Out Boy lyrics make my heart skip. "Bold choice."

"First pair I ever touched." He drops to his knee like he's swearing allegiance to my pussy. "You bet your sweet ass I'm going with these." He holds the cotton open. "Step in, Squirt."

The graze of his fingers blaze a trail fire up my calf mapping every sensitive spot he discovered last night, as I follow his command. When he hits the back of my knee, I almost collapse.

"Getting wobbly there?"

The cocky bastard knows exactly what he's doing.

"Dream on, penetration man." But my voice catches as his thumb circles my inner thigh.

He grins at my little flamingo friend. "Morning, Otis." He bumps fists with my tattoo like they're best bros now. "Looking sharp today, my man."

My heart does this weird flip-flop thing that has nothing to do with his proximity to my lady bits and everything to do with how fucking adorable he is.

"Your brain's going a mile a minute up there." His

breath fans hot against my hip, sending sparks shooting straight to my core. "But you've got this, Holly. You're a fucking force of nature."

The cotton drags higher, his knuckles grazing places that make me gasp. His teeth scrape the valley between my thigh and I swear I see stars.

"Chance…" It comes out more whimper than warning.

"They won't know what hit them." His hands smooth over my ass, adjusting the fit with way more attention than necessary. His fingers trace the lyrics spanning across my butt.

"Actually…" His palm cracks against my right cheek, the sting shooting straight to my clit. "These don't do you justice." He kneads the spot where he smacked, all possessive and shit. "You're so much more…"

I grip his shoulders as he rises, his body pressing into mine like he can't help himself. His fingers trail over the words again, each touch stealing my breath.

He kisses me hard and fast, leaving me dizzy. "Go be more than they bargained for." He steps back and pats my ass, that infuriating smirk tugging at his lips. His eyes darken as I square my shoulders and lift my chin.

He likes what I do to him as much as I like what he does to me.

Game on, soldier boy. Game on.

The heavy library doors loom before me, their frosted glass panels revealing faint shadows within. My father's confident profile is unmistakable. Beside him, Blake's shorter frame shifts restlessly, wrapped in smug confidence.

I adjust my blazer, the crisp fabric steadying under my fingertips. My manifestation underwear holds the line, acting like my personal battle cry.

Hell yes, I am.

Pushing open the doors, I stride in like I own the room—because by the end of this, I might as well. Blake's head snaps up, his smirk faltering before he reassembles his facade. My father turns, and for the first time in… maybe ever, surprise flickers across his face.

"Holly?" His voice edges with confusion as he glances between Blake and me. "What are you doing here?"

I set my laptop on the polished table keeping my movements calm and deliberate. "Same as you, Dad. Pitching to Vaultress Global."

Blake leans back, smirk stretching wider. "Playing with the big boys today?"

My lips curve into a razor-sharp smile. "Funny thing about big boys"—I meet his gaze head-on—"they usually don't need to hack into laptops to keep up with the girls."

The color drains from Blake's face, his smirk turning brittle. My father's frown deepens. "What is she talking about?"

"Nothing," Blake interjects quickly—too quickly, voice tight.

Before my father can press further, the door swings open. Ethan Kendrick strides in—tech genius turned reluctant CEO. Hair too long to be conventional, curls over his collar despite his suit. There's something unpolished about him—an edge that makes me think of well-worn jeans, flannel rolled to the elbows, and easy laughter over good beer.

He's younger than most CEOs I've worked with, but most noticeable is his barely restrained energy. Slightly abrupt movements, eyes darting and scanning faces. He's sharp and chaotic—too much.

Luckily, I speak his language.

The tension in my gut eases a fraction.

He doesn't waste time on pleasantries, his gaze sweeping the room. "Good morning. What are the chances, McAdams and McAdams?"

My lips twitch. "Yes, what are the chances, Dad?"

Ethan's eyebrows shoot up. "Wait—you all know each other?"

"Hi, I'm Holly McAdams. And this is my father, William McAdams."

Recognition flickers in his eyes as he shakes my

hand. "I saw the same last names, but assumed if you were related, you'd be on the same side."

"Yes, that does seem like the natural order of things, doesn't it?" The irony is subtle—just enough to keep Blake squirming.

"Well, how about we get started? Ladies first."

"Not at all. Let them show me how it's done."

Blake's all too eager to go first, and skids in all flash and no substance. He tosses buzzwords like confetti—streamlining, synergy, leveraging market dynamics. Corporate spaghetti thrown at walls. There's polish, but no soul. No depth.

My father speaks next. His tone shifts—steady, conservative, predictable. His decades of experience shine through, but the approach feels tired. He leans heavily on Blake to inject "youthful energy" into the proposal, only highlighting how formulaic it is.

Ethan nods along, expression polite but unreadable. Not a flicker of real interest. "Thank you. It's... comprehensive." His hesitant assessment is detached.

No spark. No excitement.

I can fix that.

Blake shoots me a smug look to conceited to even recognize he screwed the pooch. My father watches me carefully, his expression harder to read.

Time to jump start this meeting and show the old man just what he's missing.

When Ethan gestures for me to begin, I don't dive into charts. Instead, I slide my laptop away and lean forward. "What inspired the name Vaultress Global?"

The question catches him off guard. His posture shifts, something raw flickering across his face—pride mixed with vulnerability.

"It was my great-grandmother. She was a cryptographer during World War II. Worked in intelligence, not that you could find out much about her." His affectionate smile slips. "They didn't exactly give women credit for their accomplishments back then."

Don't look at your father… don't look at your father… don't look at your father…

"I'm sure she had plenty to say about that."

His eyes light up with easy laughter. "She did. Often punctuated by a middle finger." His voice lowers, laced with pride and sadness. "She used to say I wasn't out of step—I was just ahead of the beat."

I let his words hang in the air, watching the tension ease from his shoulders.

Has anyone ever asked him his why? I'm willing to bet not.

"Ethan, let's talk about maximizing your resources to live up to and honor what you've built—change the world, but ultimately, let's make sure your grandmother doesn't have one of those middle fingers aimed at you…"

He cracks a smile, the kind that makes me believe he's holding back a laugh.

Good.

I turn to my first slide: Conservative: Steady & Secure. "This option is for stability. Low-risk investments, gradual growth. Reliable, predictable, resilient against market shifts."

His fingers tap softly against the table—subtle, but I notice. His mind is already moving forward.

Next slide: Moderate: Smart & Strategic. "Now, if you're willing to take calculated risks, we move into the moderate plan. A blend of conservative and ambitious investments—emerging markets, growth stocks, ETFs. Balance between innovation and security."

Ethan tilts his head, attention sharpening. "Emerging markets. Which ones specifically?"

"AI-driven cybersecurity and renewable energy. Both volatile, yes, but at the forefront of global innovation. With the right timing, massive opportunities for long-term growth."

His tapping stops, focus locked on me. There it is—the shift I waited for.

Finally, my last slide: Aggressive: Full Throttle. "For companies ready to push the envelope, this plan focuses on high-growth, high-reward opportunities. Small-cap stocks, renewable energy, disruptive tech—these are the arenas where leaders emerge."

Ethan's posture shifts completely. He leans forward, elbows on the table, full attention locked on me. "Disruptive tech. You're talking about risk-heavy investments."

"Exactly. But not reckless ones. This isn't about throwing money at every shiny innovation—it's about identifying game-changers before they hit the mainstream. Companies with potential to redefine industries. Like Vaultress has."

The corner of his mouth quirks up—the first hint of a smile. "And you think you can identify those game-changers?"

I meet his gaze head-on. "I know I can. Because I don't just look at numbers—I look at people. Their decisions, vision, grit. That's what makes or breaks an investment, what Vaultress needs to stay ahead. This plan isn't for the faint of heart, but neither is your company—or your great-grandmother."

Ethan leans back, lips curving into an almost amused smile. "Bold wins," he murmurs.

"Bold wins," I echo. "But only when paired with precision. That's where I come in."

The room falls silent. Ethan studies me, thumbs tapping together as if weighing every word. Finally, a glint appears in his eye. "You've given me a lot to think about."

He glances briefly at my father and Blake, both unnervingly quiet. My father's expression is neutral, but his gaze lingers thoughtfully.

Ethan rises. "I'll meet with my team and follow up during cocktails tonight on my decision."

As I gather my materials, my father catches my eye. He gives the faintest nod—subtle, almost imperceptible. But for him, it might as well be a standing ovation.

I don't let it show. I adjust my blazer, nod politely to Ethan, and walk out with my head high. Behind me, Blake mutters under his breath, but it's just noise.

This time, I don't need anyone's approval. I already know I'm the one they can't afford to lose.

29

Holly

The great room pulses with anticipation, holiday music drifting through speakers while fires roar with a soothing snap and pop. Flames dance in twin fireplaces, adding warmth to the holiday ambiance. Through the windows, ski trails zigzag down the mountain like ribbons of light against the darkness.

Congregated at the bar, our family monopolizes one whole end in hushed conversation. My father keeps stealing glances at me, his face completely unreadable.

I have to wonder if it has anything to do with Blake leaving less than an hour after the presentations.

Chance smiles at me from behind his drink, a secretive smile meant only for me.

It's the smile that says, *That's my woman right there, I love her, and she's mine.* A smile I've never seen on him before. I'm willing to bet it's new, created for me, and only for me. The same one he gave me at the Shred Shack when he whispered *hi* like the word itself carried the weight of something more.

Everything about those two letters—what they say, what they leave unsaid—pulls me under. Once there, he delivered *my Holly* like a one-two punch, short-circuiting everything: lungs forgotten, knees buckling, heart on the verge of full rebellion.

Maybe today he'll say it again, only this time it won't be a whispered endearment tucked away from prying eyes.

It'll be out loud, unapologetic, and in front of everyone.

A TKO for the ages, and I'll be the one flat on the mat.

I smile back, keeping it subtle and not dialed to grab the hammer and let's ride, when I catch a glimpse of Ethan making his way through the room with his family in tow—a wife and three kids.

My heart knocks hard, a lump climbing right into my throat.

Nope. No freaking out.

Chance spots him too and shoots me a wink steadying me when my confidence wobbles on a broken heel.

And suddenly, I wish I'd already told him that I love him too. Because when I finally say it, I don't want it to be tangled up in timing, circumstance, or anything else. I want it to be about him.

About us.

Ethan's son squeals, and all eyes turn to them just as Ethan saves his toddler from a near face-plant.

Gone is the man from the presentation. Here he's an affable dad, still buzzing with the same energy but channeled in a much different direction.

He's the picture of casual in blue jeans and flannel rolled up to the elbows over a black t-shirt. Not in the forced sense common with tourists, but more a natural return to his roots.

Called it.

He's layer built on unexpected layer—the grandmother's influence no doubt—adding another level of appeal to working with him. One that speaks right to my spirit—that until this week, I had yet to fully embrace.

His oldest, a girl who looks to be around six, clutches his hand while his wife balances their infant daughter against her hip. Their toddler son trails behind, more interested in the massive tree than our gathering.

"Sorry for the delay," Ethan says, taking his son's hand before he can race off. "Someone needed an emergency diaper change, and I lost rock, paper, scissors."

"Daddy always loses," his daughter announces with the brutal honesty only kids can deliver.

"That's because Mommy's the mastermind and I'm just the guy who makes epic PB&Js." He grins, completely at ease with this admission.

I bite back a smile, something warm unfurling in my chest at their easy dynamic. At how neither of them seems concerned about who does what, just that it gets done.

At how when he's in dad mode, he's a dad and in the moment. No signs of the CEO to be found.

His little girl will be so much better for it.

My father makes his way over as the rest of our family takes a few steps back. It's just far enough to give us a bit of privacy and still hear the highlights.

A part of me wants to pause. *Just—whatever happens here, this is it.* This whole chase is over. I'll have all the answers, whether or not they hurt.

Ethan turns to me, his expression shifting to business mode, though his son is now using him as a jungle gym. "About your presentation…"

I'll never be able to go back to a time when I didn't feel this—this pull, this ache—the safety of uncertainty, because at least it wasn't guaranteed disappointment.

My stomach pitches—not quite dropping, not exactly soaring, but twisting sideways, like I'm stuck on a tilt-a-whirl I didn't ask to ride.

Ethan catches his son mid-break for the tree, barely missing a beat as he continues. "I've seen a lot of strategies," he says, setting the kid back on solid ground without losing his train of thought. "But what you showed us today? That wasn't just innovation—it was revolution. The way you mapped those transition paths…" He shakes his head, almost incredulous.

"Transition paths?" My dad cuts in, his voice sharp, with an air of authority he lacks the awareness to recognize is out of place.

Ethan's eyes snap to my father's, all intense focus. "The full plans she turned over to accompany her presentation, giving us a chance for deeper review," he says, his tone firm but measured. "You know, the ones that left my CFO speechless. And when the shock wore off"—Ethan glances briefly at his daughter with a wry smile—"I think he might've believed in you-know-who again."

A light laugh bubbles up from my chest before I can stop it, easing the knot that's been lodged there all day.

There's no way I'm losing. Not today.

"I would have been happy to provide a more detailed breakdown for you to review if that's what you wanted," my father begins.

Ethan scans the room, his tone shifting, leaning into the authority he carried earlier today. "It's what I needed. Only I didn't know it until she handed it to me."

I glance at my dad. For once, he's not the one steering the conversation. And the weight of that realization only fuels me further.

"The world is moving too fast to keep doing it the old-school way," I say quietly, in the same way I tried to be part of my father's conversation the other day, only to be dismissed at every turn.

"Exactly, and those who don't adapt will lose relevance. You're the first analyst we've found who's not only thinking ahead, but also looking at people and not just the company as a whole."

"And I don't do anything halfway."

"Traditional methods would have me locked into one approach and weeks if not months of headaches planning how to pivot. But your daughter just offered up a chess master's playbook of moves and countermoves." He smiles then and offers his hand. "So, Ms. McAdams, that's checkmate. Bold wins."

Victory is a rush of blood charging through me until I'm dizzy with the force of it.

I took control. Delivered. Forced my father to see me.

"I'll make sure you don't regret it," I say as I shake his hand, fighting to stay in the moment when a dull roar flares to life in my head, growing louder with each passing second and new revelation.

In forcing my father to see me, I see myself clearly now too.

And victory doesn't taste the way I expected.

Ethan's little boy lets out a wail that has even the cool, calm, and collected CEO wincing. "So on that shrill note, I'll be in touch next week. My team wants to meet you in person. My assistant will hammer out the details with you for whatever fits best in your schedule. Sound good?"

"Yes, sure. Absolutely. Great." The words should be enthusiastic, but instead, I'm breathless and fighting for balance as everything I thought I knew about what I thought I wanted pitches on record-setting stormy seas.

Ethan shakes my father's hand then, and they exchange words I can't hear over the new reality thundering through my head.

A reality that changes everything.

Ethan and his wife steer their kids to the tree, leaving my father standing before me. Finally taking a good hard look at me.

And from his expression, seeing what's been in front of him all along.

His face is calm, almost self-effacing, with a slight dip of the chin speaking volumes without a single word. "Sounds like your old man has had this wrong the whole time—sounds like the company could use a leader like you."

It's everything I thought I wanted. I should take it. Old me would have taken it. Pre-Chance me would have called it an epic victory.

Chance's gaze travels over me, patiently waiting with a secret smile as if he already knows what I'm about to say. And he probably does. Because he sees me in ways no one ever has.

"I don't want it." In my head the words are scary, but out loud, they're... freedom.

The chatter around us dies on my refusal.

Charlie chokes on her champagne. Eve smacks her back while simultaneously giving me a thumbs-up.

"What?" Nick's voice cuts through the silence, his jaw slack. He looks at me like I'm some unsolvable equation, a missing piece to a puzzle he's just now realizing isn't whole.

And he's right—from the outside looking in, I'm not whole—even when, for the first time, I actually am.

But not for any of the reasons he can possibly come up with.

It's the piece he doesn't know exists for me.

Chance.

Chance, who believes in me every second of every day and reinforces what I've known all along.

Chance, who saw my hyper-focus on the goal and knew I might miss the bigger picture, kind of like he did.

Chance, who believes my talent is bigger than any inherited legacy.

Chance, who knows fathers should clean up their own messes and children are meant to shatter expectations, not be weighed down by them.

"You've always wanted it," my father says, like maybe I've forgotten my lifelong mission.

"I thought I did." The words come easier than expected. "But I don't want to spend my life constantly having to convince employees I'm competent. I don't want to clean up after you, Dad. I'm sorry—I... I don't say this to be cruel. I really don't. But you've made a mess. It's not my job to clean it up. I deserve better."

He studies me as though I'm speaking a language he's never been taught.

Like I'm a puzzle he's suddenly desperate to solve.

But that's not my problem.

I'm good with being a puzzle. Let him stew over the pieces.

Nick studies me with that protective, overbearing intensity I've come to love—and also wish he'd tone the hell down. I'm not a kid anymore, no matter how much he wants to wrap me in bubble wrap and guard me from the world.

"You're sure about this, Hols?" Nick says, his voice careful and measured. "Because you've never thought anything could be better than…" His words slow, his eyes narrowing as it finally dawns on him that I'm not looking at him.

I hear him. I really do. His voice is there, saying something protective and brotherly, probably full of good intentions.

But it's nothing more than background noise now, fading into the hum of the bar.

"I found something better…"

Leaning against the mahogany like it's his throne, is my future. All sixteen pockets of unapologetic cargo glory and cocky confidence with a lopsided grin that screams, *Take a good look, guys; that's my Holly.*

It's not all cockiness, though. There's relief written on his shoulders, a looseness that wasn't there before like he finally exhaled after holding his breath for years. The man who's made a career of doing the right thing— even when it meant doing the hardest, most self-sacrificing thing imaginable—is no longer locked behind a promise eating him alive.

Something I hate that I guilted him into, even if it did lead us here.

"I've never been more sure of anything." I smile at him, my heart steady. "Well, maybe one thing."

Don't get me wrong, there's still plenty of cocky on display. Enough to have me rolling my eyes so hard I'm surprised they don't fall out of my head. He's putting on a masterclass in *I told you so* and he knows it.

And damn him, it's working.

"Well, Squirt," he drawls, amusement dripping from every word, "care to share with the class?"

Nick's brow furrows. "What? Because you've always…" Nick's gaze swings to Chance before coming back to me. "Whoa—wait. Now wait a damn minute!"

Nick goes from frantic to *aw, hell no* in under five seconds. That might be a record for my brother.

"And here," Eve narrates, her phone tracking the unfolding chaos, "we witness the rare sight of a bro code violation in its natural habitat. Note the protective male's increasing distress as he realizes his own tactical error."

"You're turning down the company for the guy who rage-kissed me under the mistletoe?" Nick's voice rises with the incredulity of a man who just caught the last train to Wrong Conclusion Junction.

"Seriously, Nick? That's what you're taking from this?" I pinch the bridge of my nose, praying for divine intervention—or at least a lightning bolt to take him out of his misery. "I've never given up anything for a man, and you suddenly think I'm going to start now?"

Charlie snorts into her freshly refilled champagne glass, eyes sparkling with amusement. "Don't worry, Hols. I'll reboot him later. Maybe clear his browser history while I'm at it."

"The male appears conflicted," Eve continues, "torn between protective instincts and the awareness of his own hypocrisy. Note the subtle tick in his jaw—a sure sign of impending surrender."

Chance pushes off the bar with a laugh and heads straight for me like it's the most natural thing in the world. Like this moment has been written in the stars for years.

He effortlessly tucks me against his side, into him—the place I fit.

The place I belong.

And instead of his usual habit of playing with my hair, he threads his fingers through with purpose, curling around the back of my neck. It's a move that leaves not one goddamn question in the room about the super-secret network we've built this week.

Deep and possessive, his kiss tastes like promise and possibility—and nothing like cleaning up someone else's mess.

"I need therapy," Nick announces to no one in particular. "Man on the ground, my ass. And how much dirty work are we talking, Chance? You know what, don't answer that. You lied to me. A lot."

Chance stiffens next to me, but it's not anger, it's that stoic, responsible soldier showing up to take responsibility. "I did. And you know just what that's like, don't you?"

"Subject attempts a direct confrontation," Eve narrates, "only to be thwarted by his enemy's superior knowledge of his own infractions."

"Not quite the same though, is it? I crossed the line,

but I didn't lie to you about it. So what's your point?" Nick demands.

"I had a choice. My loyalty to you or her—I chose her. And I'd do it again—I'll do it every time."

The tone of his voice is a heady combination of resolute and authoritative. His loyalty—almost all promise, with a dash of threat—heals the ache of a lifetime of being second, third, and sometimes fourth choice, still lodged in my heart.

"I'm sorry that I had to do it to you, of all people. But I'm not sorry I did it. It's what you would expect from the man who loves her, Nick. Don't hold it against me that I had to betray *you* to do it."

He can't argue the logic, and he knows it. The truth of that is right there in Nick's eyes. "Fuck."

"They did," Eve says at the speed of mischief.

"Easy, Eve," Charlie says with a snort. "Bruising the dick for fun is one thing, breaking it… well, it's my dick, so let's not overseason the steak again."

Nick scrubs a hand through his hair and blows out a breath. "I need a drink. Or two. Probably ten. You're buying, Chance. Until I'm dead."

"Worth it," Chance says as he drops a lingering kiss on my lips.

"Don't sweat it. Keep this up and you won't even have to tap into the savings," Eve says.

Our families' laughter blends into the background until I barely hear it.

Because I've found my place. It's not in my father's shadow or his legacy.

It's right here, in my own Hallmark movie directed by Satan in the form of possessed mistletoe. My once upon a time Holly style—a storm, a confession, and a brother's best friend walk into a bar…

If the bar is in Narnia, keep an eye out for the sock and the Tupperware lid.

Fuck the pride that ran off with my lapse in judgment. Narnia can keep it.

Because my past mistakes have nothing on the triumphs ahead.

All with a man who doesn't just want me to plan the dinner parties—he wants to throw them with me—and maybe execute a few of his own. He likes a good power trip every now and then.

But we're both doing the dishes.

Unless I smash them.

Gotta keep it interesting.

Either way, we're doing it together.

EPILOGUE

Holly & CHANCE & Holly

Because boss bitches get the first and last word.

One Year Later

HOLLY

Look at that man over there.

Good God.

Cargo pants?

Check.

A Henley that subtly molds around his pecs?

Fucking check.

Dog tags that do double duty as a handle, making Chance feral with lust?

Motherfucking check.

He shoots me a wink from where he's leaning against the bar, all easy confidence, chatting with Everett's uncle Seth and—surprisingly—his own dad.

Chance had been back for less than a week after the

annual family Christmas trip when his dad called him up to meet for drinks. Before the night was through, his father dropped two bombshell apologies: first, for the colossal Noelle-shaped landmine he dropped, and second, for making Chance feel like marriage was the price of his approval.

Apparently, skeletons started sliding out of his father's closet faster than a busted Jenga tower.

So many that I ended up picking them up—the boys, not the skeletons—because not only could they not drive, but they were a tangle of hugs and half-slurred "I love you, mans."

Neither of them remembers that part. *Supposedly.*

I call bullshit.

"Not bad work for just a year. You did good," Everett says, sliding a hot chocolate with Bailey's across the counter like it's a peace offering.

"That's all them." I lean on the counter and give him a pointed look. "Besides, I'm not the one up to the mistletoe fuckery. Decide to take the year off?"

His startled eyes meet mine. "You knew?"

"Not until a few days ago when I spotted you trying to execute a sneak attack on your uncle Seth."

"Yeah, sorry about that. Your mom was a good sport about it, though."

Of course, she was. She totally used it to get my dad to up his game. What game? I don't want to know. It's bad enough I recognize the smiles and the content look only *that* kind of exhaustion can bring.

Everett rolls his eyes. "You two were exhausting. I've never worked so hard at matchmaking in my life."

"You know…" I stir my drink and watch him, looking for all the little clues. "You seem to be good at seeing what people need."

He winks. "It's a gift."

"But who takes care of what you need?"

The smile that naturally lights his eyes slips, but before I can go there, my phone buzzes, Eve's message lighting up the screen like a red alert.

EVE

Alright, team. The parents are three drinks in and talking about playing Never Have I Ever 😈

ME

Oh no

CHARLIE

Oh yes

NICK

Absolutely not. Shut it down.

EVE

Too late. Your mom just pulled out the cards, and my Mom's pouring Fireball. For the record, this one's not on me

ME

Since when do they even know drinking games

CHARLIE

TikTok. My Mom's been watching "family game night" videos

NICK

Can we just go back to last year when all
I had to do was worry about Chance
kissing me again?

CHANCE

If you were looking for another kiss, all
you had to do is say so.

CHARLIE

No. I'm pregnant and horny. I need Nick
uncontaminated and ready to service me
at all times.

CHANCE

New rule. Horny is outlawed in group
chats.

CHARLIE

So that's code for you're not getting
bone tonight, Holly. Cause Chance's 🦴
just died.

NICK

Bone… also outlawed in group chats.

EVE

Get it together people! They've got that
look. You know the one. Like they're
about to traumatize us "for fun"

ME

Avoid anything involving the boathouse
or suspicious bruises from the 90s.

NICK

What the hell happened in the 90s?

EVE

Heard there were tabs and slots
involved. Don't ask questions you don't
want answered.

NICK

I'm never getting on any of the family
boats again

From the great room, the distinct sound of shot glasses clinking makes my stomach drop. Mrs. McAllister's voice carries that dangerous enthusiasm that spells disaster. "It'll be perfect! We can all bond!"

CHANCE

You over seasoned them ONCE and now
we're living in your personally crafted
hell.

CHANCE

Not my favorite sister right now.

CHARLIE

I could fake labor?

NICK

Don't you dare. We're saving that card
for real emergencies.

CHANCE

Like what?

EVE

Battle stations, people. If they start
telling college stories, it's every man for
himself.

"Kids!" Mrs. McAllister's voice rings out. "Time for a new tradition!"

MAMA MCADAMS HAS BEEN ADDED TO THE CHAT.
MAMA MCALLISTER HAS BEEN ADDED TO THE CHAT.

NICK

DAMMIT EVE!

CHANCE

One year ago, if someone told me I'd be watching my father laugh over beers with Nick, discussing ski season like old friends, I'd have checked their field report for accuracy and questioned their mental state. The man who turned every breath into a tactical assessment is just… being a dad.

Talk about mission failure in the best possible way.

That first real conversation felt like defusing an IED —precise movements, raw nerves, both of us terrified of triggering the wrong wire. Him admitting he'd screwed up was just the start. We're still navigating the terrain, stumbling sometimes, but watching him now? It's like observing a completely different target.

And Holly…

My eyes track her always. Right now, she's across the

room, head thrown back in laughter at something Everett said. She's incendiary—all controlled chaos and brilliant strategy, commanding every inch of space she claims. The sight hits me square in the chest, the familiar ache that defies physics landing with military precision.

She doesn't just succeed. She obliterates expectations.

Setting her plans in motion put Vaultress Global in the news five times alone just based on their unprecedented growth and bold, strategic expansion.

Every report ended with the same burning question: What's their secret weapon?

My Holly.

That's always the answer. Not that she's telling. Or Ethan for that matter. Nope. They're both content to stay head down and full speed ahead.

Let everyone wonder. She doesn't want the recognition. Nor does she need it. Not anymore.

This past year, watching her storm through the industry, forcing people to see what I've always known was there—it's been like watching lightning strike in slow motion.

Beautiful. Powerful.

Absolutely unstoppable.

It's not just her intelligence, though that's something to behold. It's her heart. The way she takes care of everyone around her, even when she thinks no one's watching.

Yeah, I've never been more certain of anything.

The conversations that used to tangle me in knots, the choices that felt impossible—they're clear now.

My fingers brush the velvet box in my sixteenth pocket. A tiny piece of forever just waiting for deployment. For her.

"You good?" Nick materializes at my shoulder, fresh beer in hand and that look in his eye like he's running a tactical assessment.

"Better than good."

He nods slowly, taking a pull from his beer as his gaze drifts to Holly. "She's something, isn't she?"

I can't help the laugh that escapes. "You have no idea."

There's no tension between us now, no weight of history or unspoken warnings. Just understanding that we fought hard to earn.

Nick claps my shoulder. "You've done good, man. Proud of you."

The words settle easy now, natural as breathing. "Thanks, brother."

Across the room, Holly catches my eye. That little smirk tugs at her lips—the one that says she's already run three scenarios ahead of me and has contingency plans for each one.

Everything is clicking into place.

And soon, when I ask her the question burning in my pockets, everything will be perfect.

Because the mistletoe might have started this, but I'm going to finish it.

I pocket my phone and head in Holly's direction. At

least whatever psychological warfare our mothers have planned, we're facing it together.

We meet at one of the overstuffed recliners, where she settles on my lap.

Nick's mom clears her throat and pulls a deck of cards out of nowhere, her smile nothing short of predatory. "Never Have I Ever?"

"I'm gonna need so much more alcohol," Holly mutters against my neck. "We can't unknow any of this."

I stroke her spine, to soothe her or me, who the hell knows. "They're our parents… how bad can it actually get?"

Twenty minutes later, we're in a circle, drinks in hand. The parents are three shots deep, and things are spiraling. Fast.

And I regret ever uttering the words about how bad it can get to Holly.

"Never have I ever…" Mrs. McAdams pauses dramatically. "…had sex in public."

Every single parent drinks.

"Jesus Christ," Nick mutters, clutching his glass like it's the only thing keeping him tethered to reality.

"The boathouse wasn't public," Mrs. McAdams protests. "It was… semi-private."

Boathouse—right out of the fucking gate.

"Ellen!" My mom gasps, looking scandalized. "That was you?"

Eve, ever the documentarian, pulls out her phone.

"Here we observe the mating habits of the wild boomers, establishing territory through strategic—"

"Never have I ever," Nick interrupts desperately before flipping his card. He closes his eyes and blows out a breath. "…gotten caught watching porn."

Oh, that had to hurt.

Good.

Bout time he got zinged for once.

My mother's hand shoots up. "Oh! That reminds me of when we found Chance's browser history—"

Jesus Christ.

The whiskey burns as I choke it down. "We are NOT discussing my browser history. MOVE ON." How the hell did his zing find me at the speed of fucking light.

Besides, I watch my porn a whole lot differently these days. I'd like to think my tastes have matured. Refined. Aged like a fine wine.

Actually, I watch hers.

With her.

While she bosses me around.

I definitely have a kink for CEO McAdams unabashedly watching the dirty while she makes me follow her every command.

"Never have I ever gotten caught grinding on someone's leg while dancing," Eve continues, her reign of terror nowhere near complete.

"That was ONE TIME at the lodge Christmas party," my mother protests. "And we thought the supply closet was empty—"

"I QUIT," Nick announces to no one in particular. "I'm actually quitting life."

"Never have I ever," Charlie continues, clearly drunk on power now, but only power since she's drinking ginger ale. "Called out the wrong name during sex."

"That was YOUR fault," Mrs. McAdams points accusingly at her husband. "Who grows a mustache identical to their father's?"

"WAIT A GODDAMN MINUTE?" Nick's voice cracks. "GRANDPA?"

Holly's practically crying with laughter now, her face nestled against my chest as she curls into me.

The one thing that could make it better is if we were alone and she was wearing my shirt.

She tips her face up to mine, eyes bright, that pretty mouth that looks fucking phenomenal working my cock, smiling up at me.

My heart does that wild flip again—the one that says she owns every piece of me. Cupping her chin, I can only stare down at her and wonder how the hell I got lucky enough for her to choose me.

I nod toward the door. Time to give her the gift burning a hole in my sixt—

A crack thunders through the great hall as the lodge doors slam open, wind and snow gusting inside like a freaking movie trailer. Sierra storms in, all pale-blond hair, fury, and a vintage camera slung around her neck like a weapon. She looks like she's on a warpath, and I'm pretty sure Everett's the target.

It was only a matter of time.

And can anyone say, fucking finally? Jesus.

"Everett Morgan, you absolute bastard!"

Everyone freezes.

Everett straightens, his easy grin shifting into something sharper, something I've never quite seen before, and I've pretty much seen it all with him.

"Ah, Sierra," he says, calm as ever, but there's a spark in his voice, like he's been expecting this. "You got the application with the renovation plans I take it?"

"Renovations?" she spits, stomping toward him like she's ready to throw hands. "You're destroying the historic integrity of—"

"The lodge needs updating—"

"That's not updating—that's personal."

Sierra slaps her palms on the bar and climbs right up in his face.

On her hands and knees.

Not quite the power position she thinks it is. More like he's going to get all sorts of ideas with her up there, but hey, it's probably exactly what they need.

She jabs a finger into Everett's chest, her fury reaching a fever pitch. "I've documented every historic detail of this lodge. You can't just—"

Everett finally notices his audience. His eyes flick to the rest of us, then back to Sierra. The spark in his expression shifts to something darker, quieter, like he's drawing the line in the snow.

"Why don't we discuss this somewhere more private?" he says, his voice low.

Sierra doesn't budge. "Oh no, Everett. If you're

going to ruin this place, I want everyone to witness every shitty move and never let you forget."

The lodge might survive the renovations, but this? This feels like the kind of storm you don't see coming until it's right on top of you.

Holly nudges me. "Should we step in?"

"Not a chance. You want someone to interrupt our foreplay?" I shake my head and rest my chin on her hair. "Let 'em sort it out."

"I'm not sure they'll survive."

Brushing a kiss over her temple, my laugh rumbling over her skin elicits a shiver I'm all too familiar with. "Everett's met his match. She'll keep him in line."

As Everett opens his mouth to argue, Sierra snaps a photo just inches from his face—flash and all—and hops off the bar muttering something about documenting every insult to the lodge's history.

"Well, at least we'll have pictures of the carnage," Holly says with a laugh.

"Professional grade, too."

As Everett turns back to the bar, he catches us watching him. He raises an eyebrow, the grin sliding back into place like armor. "Something on your mind, McAdams?"

"Yeah," she calls back. "Just wondering how long it's gonna take her to make you eat that smug little smile."

His laugh is easy, but there's a flicker of something deeper in his eyes. "Careful, Holly. You're dangerously close to underestimating me."

HOLLY

The hay crinkles under the tarp as Chance tugs me down beside him, my back pressed to his chest. The wagon creaks with our movement, a familiar sound that sends heat blooming in my cheeks.

"Earbuds?" he asks, his breath warm against my ear.

"Always." I pass him one, slipping the other into my ear. Fall Out Boy fills the silence between us, kicking off my playlist, and I can't help but smile.

His hand slides down to my hip. "I have something for you."

"Is it in one of your sixteen pockets?"

"Actually…" He leans back with his arms crossed behind his head, giving me that devastating grin that still makes my heart skip. "Every one of them. You have to find them all."

"All sixteen?"

"Yup." He pops the *P* with infuriating smugness. "Better get started, Squirt."

The first pocket yields something soft and silky. I pull it out, squinting in the low light. "Are these…"

"Manifestation panties." His voice drops low, sending shivers down my spine. "Check the word."

Written across the back in his familiar scrawl: SQUIRT.

Of course this would be the pair I find first.

"Don't stop now, Squirt." he prompts when I just stare at them.

The next pocket produces another pair: OTIS.

By the sixth pocket, my hands are shaking. The words come out of order, and I piece them together as I go: MY RIDE OR DIE.

"Chance…"

He jerks his chin and winks. "Keep going, baby."

Eight pockets in: SQUIRT OTIS MY RIDE OR DIE HONEST FLAMINGO.

My heart pounds against my ribs as I reach for the thirteenth pocket: LET'S.

Fourteen: YOU'RE.

Fifteen: ME?

I pause at the final pocket, my fingers trembling. Chance's warm hand covers mine. "Together?" he asks softly.

I nod, not trusting my voice.

We pull out the last pair… MARRY.

"Holly." His voice is rough with emotion as he cups my face in his hands. "Squirt, you're my ride or die." His gaze drops to my mouth the way it always does. Only he doesn't linger this time. This time he meets my eyes again, and there's a sliver of vulnerability there.

"Let's make an honest flamingo out of Otis." His thumb brushes over my lip. "Marry me?"

Tears blur my vision as I launch myself at him, knocking him back into the hay. "Yes. God, yes."

His kiss is fierce and tender all at once, full of promises and forever.

When he finally pulls back, he's grinning like an idiot. "Good, because there's more."

Cocooned under a tarp in a bed of hay, I open the single most gorgeous diamond I've ever seen.

My heart lurches, caught somewhere between disbelief and a wild, reckless kind of hope. My fingers tremble as I trace the pear-cut diamond—sharp on one side, soft and curved on the other. It's beautiful, impossibly delicate like the whole thing could tip out of its setting with one wrong move.

But it doesn't.

The intricate metalwork twists around the stone, clinging to it with a kind of fierce determination as if it knows exactly how precious it is. Every ridge, every groove, feels intentional like it was designed not just to hold the diamond but to honor it.

It's breathtaking. Strong and fragile all at once. And as it gleams in the light, my breath catches in my throat.

Oh God. This is real.

Slipping the ring from the box, I hook it over my index finger—because he's going to be the one to put it on me—and take his face in my hands. "I love you, soldier boy," I murmur over his mouth.

"I love you too, Squirt." He dips his head and nips at my throat as he deftly takes the ring and slides it on my ring finger.

Everything goes quiet as we stare down at the next chapter in our story. The music playing shifts as if it's been in on the plan the whole time. Only it's my playlist so that's impossible. The opening chords to "Carry You Home" drift in.

"Now," he starts, the words a gentle rumble against my collarbone as he tastes every bit of my exposed skin—pretty much his favorite way to end the day, not that I hate it. "What do you say we get started christening these new panties."

I tilt my head, tucking my cheek against his as I wait for the tickling sensation when he hits this one spot—ahhhh, yeah, that one—goosebumps dance across my skin, all the way to the roots of my hair. "All sixteen pairs?"

His growl vibrates against my skin. "We've got all night, Squirt."

"Don't call me Squirt when you're about to—oh!"

His mouth claims mine, stealing the words, the breath, everything but this—us, together, forever.

Flipping me under him, my eyes land on the hammer hooked overhead just like that night. Next to it, our mistletoe watches over us like some kind of kinky guardian angel.

Just the way it should be.

meet ECHO

Echo Grayce serves small-town steam that smells like whiskey and tastes like rebellion—where the bar's always open, the women run the show, and the chaos comes with a cherry on top. Her romances feel like a roller derby bruise you don't regret: loud, dirty, and full of women who take exactly what they want. After all, happily ever after tastes better with cocktails, sass, and a side of **sex toys & shenanigans.**

For new books, old books, tastes-great-less-filling books, signings, playlists, story boards, and so much more, go to my website.

www.EchoGrayce.com

And for the latest news, and let's face it, the announcements I will absolutely forget to put on socials, sign up for my newsletter while you're there!
Want the bangers??? Get them here
geni.us/HollyDaysBangers

Acknowledgments

It's no secret this release was the single most fucked launch of my ten-year career—forty-plus books and counting.

I was completely at the mercy of the Zon, and they made me their bitch. Anxiety has never been my thing, but this time, it kicked my whole ass.

My book was stuck for twelve days.

Twelve. Fucking. Days.

When it finally started delivering again in its entirety, it delivered the 💩 version.

To this day, the Zon has not followed through on pushing the right version. The reviews… well, let's not talk about it. I can't look at them. My dings are on the glitches and there's not one damned thing I can do about it.

Again, at the mercy of the Zon.

There was a handful of people who helped me through and kept me sane when…

I couldn't talk without crying.

I had endless chest pains to the point I thought I needed the ER.

I stayed up all hours of the night refreshing obsessively and walked around like a zombie from a severe lack of sleep.

I lost seven pounds in the first three days alone.

I spent over seventeen hours in total on the phone with techs at the Zon.

I spent endless hours managing dozens upon dozens of emails back and forth with them.

I scared the hell out of my friends. Got real quiet when I'm not quiet at all.

And to be honest, I scared myself a whole lot too.

But there were a few people who held me together…

CHRISTIANA—the insanely talented illustrator you know as Concepts by Canea, my alpha reader, my most trusted confidante, and a surprise best friend I never saw coming. Who knew finally letting go of one 💩 "best friend" would bring me the goddamned best friend pot of gold at the end of the rainbow, but here we are.

Thank you is so fucking inadequate…

Normally, these acknowledgments would be private notes, but you all need to know about this woman. She never stopped checking on me—day or night—even with a time zone difference between London and the States.

She kept me from crumbling, minute by minute, hour by hour, day by day, talking me off a lifetime's worth of ledges over the course of twelve horrendous days (and still going).

She sends me screenshots of the amazing reviews coming in because if I go look at my book and see the bad ones from this glitch, I'll spiral and never write again.

Yes, it's that crippling.

Christiana, you've taken care of me in ways I couldn't for myself, and there's no way to repay you for that. I've always been the steel spine—a stubborn pain in the ass, I've never let anyone take care of me.

So when, for the first time in my life, something sent me reeling, most of the people around me had no idea. It never occurred to them I might actually be falling apart, but you saw it. And you didn't hesitate to take action.

What was likely no big deal for you, changed everything for me 🤍

MELISSA—

Replying to that post about helping run Sacrilege was the single best thing I've done. Nothing has been the same since, thank fuck! You were the disturbance my life needed and I can confidently say that had we not become friends, I'd still likely be stuck in *that* shitty situation with that shitty human. You know the one, situation and human respectively, LOL.

You showed me repeatedly that I deserve better, and patiently waited for me to finally believe you.

You single handedly gave me the courage to break free, and the confidence to know I deserve better. Because of you, I'll never fall into the same trap again. Nor will I settle for less than I deserve in a friendship.

Then, there's the fact that I would not have Christiana in my life if it weren't for you!

And finally, you were the voice of reason and the comic relief I so desperately needed when this release went sideways. I'm telling you, your GIF game is unparalleled! I would not have made it through this with my sanity intact if it weren't for you. Thank you for everything you've done, and continue to do to make my life better… I'm pretty sure you give me a whole lot more than I give you…

HEY ASHLEY—Girl ●●
You clenched didn't you? LOL.
You have to be the most chill person I've ever met. Seriously… that's hard to do with someone like Melissa around, but damn.

Every time you come back with a super chill response,

especially during this release, my brain skids to a stop making me question if things are as bad as I think they are.

In this case, they were… there's no avoiding the truth of that. But your absolute calm pulled me out of my shit spiral for the briefest moment—a moment I desperately needed. Thank you for holding me together, prodding me, managing me (Jesus, someone has to… I don't envy you the job), and being rock solid and supportive every step of the way.

Here's to that night in July when we broke the professional ice—shattered that shit to pieces